GO FOR IT !

RC Smith

GO FOR IT !

GO FOR IT ! is a work of fiction based on a true
story. Names, characters, events, and incidents are
the product of the author's imagination or are used
fictitiously. Places and background of public events
are not always fictitious. However, the financial
crisis reported by *The New York Times* on April 4,
1973, is true.

ISBN 9781076491701

To…

My wife Marie and my daughter Becky,
for all the encouragement they gave me.

Liz Wildberger, who taught me how to write.

Robbi Sommers Bryant, who taught me how to
create a novel.

Table of Contents

Prologue

It was the beginning of the end. Financial disaster loomed in the United States, and the glorious post-World War II days of pent-up demand and economic growth fluctuated. On the horizon, a great "bear market" rumbled.

On August 15, 1971, President Richard M. Nixon announced his economic policy, a program "to create a new prosperity without war" known colloquially as the Nixon Shock. His Bretton Woods Initiative marked the first stages of the failure of the Bretton Woods System when he took the U.S. off the gold standard of fixed exchange rates established at the end of World War II. The Arab Oil Crisis followed; lines of cars and trucks surrounded every block. Almost half of the stock market value of the Dow Jones Industrial Average was lost. Unemployment surged to over ten percent.

Interest rates raged much higher, and inflation neared twenty percent in the mid-70s. Paul Volker, Chairman of the Federal Reserve Board, had not yet raised the Federal Funds interest rate to tame inflation for the 1980s.

The first index fund, established by William Fouse and John McQuown of Wells Fargo Bank, was followed by the rise of no-load mutual funds later in the decade. The future was dire. But from the bleakness, four young veterans took on the challenge and vowed to confront the way the financial services industry did business.

The life insurance business continued to evolve. Individual policies were a traditional financial product for Middle America. Around the turn of the century, the Metropolitan Life salesman made his monthly house calls to collect the dimes and quarters Mom had squirreled away in her budget envelopes in the pantry. A savings element with a cash value was added, creating Whole Life Insurance. In the mid-century, premium payments could be variable in accordance with the investment results achieved by the insurance company. In the

1960s, Equity Funding Corporation of America introduced premium financing in a program using life insurance and mutual funds; it was the only company to offer funding.

The investment industry, built on commissions, was murky; conflicts of interest prevailed. Each time a stockbroker moved a client's money between rising and falling stocks, he got a commission. The broker put the customer into a stock—commission. The stock goes down, and the broker tells his client to sell—commission. The broker puts him into another stock—commission. That stock goes either up or down, and the broker has the client sell and either take his profit or realize his loss—yet another commission.

Fred Maloney grew up in the 1950s and 60s—an era of plenty—but in 1969, he felt the frustrations this new era of change brought. For the first time, he realized he could not promise his customers a better life for their children and grandchildren.

Fred Maloney believed the financial services industry should allow customers to choose a financial product rather than have one pushed on them. The industry had created barriers preventing the sale of non-industry products. Fred intended to tear these barriers down by providing his clients with safe products geared to *their* needs.

With the availability of the new mutual funds and affordable life insurance policies, Fred thought the financial abuse should be slowed. He knew independent reps and agents could rebuff the lack of accountability in the industry if they had an alternative. Financial planning could be that alternative.

Fred knew that teaching financial advisors to educate their customers and provide a channel for their expectations was more effective than selling the company's specific products. The way the system currently worked left people vulnerable to financial exploitation. The incentives created by commissions prodded the salesman, and his primary objective became getting the sale—any sale—if he wanted to make a living.

Fred wanted to embrace a new concept for the salesman—financial planning. Rather than simply selling products to his clients, the salesman would help them plan their futures. Fred knew the industry *could* provide the guidance required. But as it stood, most salesmen preferred selling products that generated commissions.

If the salesman acted as a financial consultant rather than as a broker receiving commissions, there would be less incentive for him to switch investment products at the whim of the stock market. This conservative approach would serve a client whose primary interest was to protect his family if death or financial uncertainty occurred. Financial planning held those two objectives together—acting as a consultant to the customer and earning a commission. If the client came first, both the sales rep *and* the client could prosper.

In the banking industry, wealthy customers had the opportunity to finance the premium payments on their life insurance policies and pay the loans off later with cheaper dollars. But that door was not open to the middle class. Banks loaned money to those prosperous enough to pay the interest and repay the loans. This limited Middle America to long-term financing for their homes.

Besides real estate loans, funding utilized an administrative process of using mutual funds as security for loans to pay the premiums on life insurance policies sold by the agent. The customer expected that the premium loans would be repaid from the mutual funds that grew in value over his lifetime.

Three military pilots and a paratrooper came together to challenge the status quo and make room for Middle America's financial advancement. Fred Maloney had been a Marine pilot flying near Guantanamo Bay during the Cuban missile crisis and was comfortable taking risks. Marco Flynn, another Marine pilot and a Stanford Law graduate, helped Fred find financing to support his dream. Jim Barns, a graduate of West Point, served his time in the army and then went on to MIT where he received a master's degree. Jim would provide the energy to recruit foot soldiers for a new company. After aircraft carrier tours in the Mediterranean, Rick Taylor finished college at Notre Dame and then graduated from the Michigan Law School. Rick would help the new company get through the legal barbed wire. Their inspiring stories follow.

ACT I
The Mission

CHAPTER ONE
Time to Change

In May 1968, Fred and Peggy Maloney settled into Queen Anne chairs at their favorite cocktail table in the Pensacola Country Club. They often gathered with friends for weekend dining, either at the country club or at the Pensacola Yacht Club where Fred moored his thirty-eight-foot cabin cruiser. Both Maloneys enjoyed golfing at the club and cruising on Pensacola Bay. Fred had just returned from a two-day trip to Montgomery, Alabama, where he enjoyed eighteen holes of golf with two of his clients.

He returned home after the match to exchange his golfing clothes for a dinner jacket. He then took Peggy to the country club for a quiet evening. Once they arrived, they greeted friends then selected a cocktail table near the large window overlooking the tenth tee. Peggy sipped her delicious Rob Roy and jiggled the ice cubes until she could reach the long-stemmed cherry.

As she placed her cocktail glass down on the table, Peggy turned to Fred. "I saw Andrea DeFay today. Since John died, she's been trying to take care of the kids *and* run that dry-cleaning business. She could use help at the cleaners but can't afford it. She's struggling, Fred—it's sad."

Fred's brow furrowed and anger flashed in his eyes. He crushed his Marlboro cigarette into the ashtray. "Damn it! John DeFay didn't have a life insurance policy. He had no plan or financial safeguards for his family. I tried to set him up with a policy, but he was stubborn. No matter how I framed it, he thought the dry cleaning and laundry business would protect Andrea and the kids. Everyone knows how much he loved to play the stock market. He must have lost everything in that latest market drop."

A tear balanced on the rim of Fred's eye. "The financial industry wants its salesmen to force its products on consumers. Every time the client

4

made a recommended change, the client paid a commission. People should learn to make their plans instead of being told what to buy. It's like working with a bully."

Aggravated, Fred shook his head and stared down at his smoldering cigarette.

Peggy realized she had ruined the mood for a delightful evening by mentioning John DeFay's demise and looked away. The high heel she balanced on her foot fell to the hardwood floor with a clunk.

"*What*?" Fred said, his tone cool.

"You're right," Peggy replied. She was always quick to follow his lead. Used to having things done the way he wanted, Fred expected others to follow his guidance.

Fred pulled another Marlborough from the pack in his shirt pocket. "I guess if I want changes in this industry, I'll have to start with myself." He clicked his lighter and lit another cigarette.

Fred remembered the times he had tried to encourage John DeFay to review his life insurance needs for his growing family. The more he thought about it, the more frustrated he became. Fred was upset with himself.

Fred didn't like to explain the orders he gave, nor apologize. His red hair, cut into a butch style, was a holdover from his days in the Marine Corps. His thin mustache often looked more brown than red, especially when he frowned. Not quite as tall as the other men he flew with, both on active duty and as a reserve pilot, Fred trained in New Orleans one weekend each month. He was the Skipper of his Marine Corps reserve squadron.

With an intense look in his eyes, Fred growled, "I repeatedly told John DeFay, 'don't play the stock market.' I tried to explain mutual funds to him—but no, he didn't have time. He refused to talk about life insurance, for himself *or* his business. I wasn't firm enough."

Fred exhaled a cloud of cigarette smoke. "I asked him to come to my office many times. 'Let's talk about your financial security' I'd say, but again, he was too busy. I should have pushed harder."

"You did the best you could, Fred. As you said, that man was stubborn. Poor Andrea." Peggy let her other shoe drop to the floor. "What can she do?"

Fred shook his head and took another sip of his scotch and water.

"You're right about bully salesmen," Peggy offered. "It's completely unfair."

Fred downed what remained of his scotch and water, slammed the glass onto the table, and got up from his chair. "I don't feel like a big dinner right now. Okay with you if we just go on home?"

***

Fred Maloney grew up in Pensacola, Florida. When first married in December 1958, he proudly introduced his bride to the local gentry in the Grand Ballroom of the Pensacola Country Club. He had finished flight training at the Forrest Sherman Field in the Pensacola Naval Air Training Command and then went on the remainder of his four years of active duty flying Marine Corps jet fighters.

Peggy's long blonde hair flowed down over her shoulders and highlighted her gentle blue eyes—eyes that had entranced Fred from the moment they met at St. Mary's, a women's college across from the male-only University of Notre Dame campus on highway US 31.

At Notre Dame, Fred met Rick Taylor. They were both taking a business class taught by Professor Shapiro during the summer session preceding their senior year. A natural bond evolved between the two men. Rick had been a Navy carrier pilot; Fred was then in the Reserve Officer Training Corps (ROTC) at Notre Dame. Fred loved to talk about flying with Rick, who had recently returned from his active duty in the Navy. Fred started his Marine Corps flight training at the Naval Air Training Command in Pensacola following graduation

Fred and three other ND students crossed the highway separating the two schools and met some of the St. Mary's girls on a football weekend. Peggy Petersen and three of her girlfriends had tickets for the game. Fred noticed Peggy's eyes catch his as they walked together around the St. Mary's campus.

At the dance following the football game, Fred and Peggy danced and held hands. The warmth enveloped them both, and a relationship began. Fred knew she was from Iowa, but he also knew that St. Mary's College was not far away from Notre Dame.

In 1962, after his active duty tour in the Marine Corps, Fred moved Peggy and their son and daughter into the Maloney nineteenth-century home in Pensacola, where Fred grew up. The house, perched alongside the eighth fairway at the Pensacola Country Club, overlooked the Gulf of Mexico. He loved to work in his yard where seasonal plants and flowers wove back and forth with the gentle Gulf breeze. In the back, Fred created a pleasant place for the children to play, and he often sat in his white, wrought iron swing to watch them, as he awaited the arrival of their third child.

Fred wanted to keep on flying, and Peggy supported him. He stayed in the Marine Corps reserves. When he was home, Fred enjoyed the peaceful view of the Gulf and the surf below where he spent many hours on his 38-foot cabin cruiser.

When recalling his childhood, a wave of emotion would rush through him. His parents and grandparents had bequeathed him a rich heritage of a love of God, country, and community. He wanted to pass on this legacy to his children. That tradition served him well in the Marine Corps.

Peggy loved their Gulf home. Welcomed by the local community, Peggy demonstrated her affection by getting involved with the local church and other activities. An active woman, Peggy became president of the alumni club of Saint Mary's College. Even so, she made sure plenty of love was bestowed on their three children, even with their father doing so much flying and traveling in his full-time insurance job. The religious stalwart of the family, Peggy made sure the children took every opportunity that local family-oriented groups provided.

Peggy put love into furnishing the old house. Both she and Fred placed antiques their parents had accumulated over a lifetime on the tables and walls. Together, the Maloneys turned a beautiful house on the golf course into a warm home. Here they planned a new world for their children.

Fred grew up around money and was used to the good things in life. A six-handicap golfer, he'd played at the club since he'd learned to caddy as a young teen—even winning an invitational tournament at the Pensacola Country Club. He loved to spend time aboard his boat and often took his family cruising in Pensacola Bay.

Fred's job also involved recruiting agents for Pioneer Life Insurance Company and representatives (reps) to sell Boston Company mutual funds sponsored by the United Express Company. He was licensed for both life insurance and securities. He tried to encourage agents he recruited to put the customer's interest first. "Unlike most life insurance companies, Pioneer Life keeps its customers' interests in mind when it designs life insurance policies," he assured his salesmen. He told reps that Boston Company had a long history of quality customer care.

Fred installed his first pension and profit-sharing plan for the employees of the Pensacola Oldsmobile dealer—the dealer where he bought an Oldsmobile '98 convertible every few years. Most of his traveling related to his business of life insurance, mutual funds, and retirement planning. Fred kept himself up to date on investments and investment products by attending local underwriter and product meetings around the Southeast.

Although Fred settled into the good life in Pensacola, his financial success wasn't enough to satisfy him. His passion focused on fixing the system in which the goals of the financial services industry were stacked against the customers. With all the knowledge that life insurance agents and investment representatives accumulated, Fred believed the industry's mission should lie in assisting customers—teaching them to develop financial plans for their families. This should be the primary function of a salesman. Even so, Fred spent most of those early days in Florida and southern Alabama selling life insurance, mutual funds, and retirement plans.

***

In late May 1969, the president of Pioneer Life Insurance Company asked Fred to join him in his office. Similar to Fred, Forrest Senf had come up through the ranks. Certificates and testimonials filled the walls of Forrest's office. He gazed at Fred across his large mahogany desk. Strands of white peeked through his neatly combed gray hair. A friendly smile graced his lips as he stubbed out a cigarette into his corporate ashtray. Fred had been selling Pioneer life insurance policies for Forrest around the southeast for the better part of a decade.

Fred lit his Marlboro and put his lighter back into his pocket. Ever since Forrest's phone call, Fred wondered what was up. Now, sitting across from Forrest, Fred said, "The company needs a spark for its product line. If Pioneer Life adds funding to its portfolio, it would be a step toward financial planning for customers. This introduces clients to long-term planning instead of another sales pitch for life insurance."

Forrest leaned back in his chair. "I don't want to discuss funding, Fred. I know Equity Funding Corporation has mixed premium financing loans into the life insurance policies it sells. But my actuaries can't make the numbers work. Equity Funding Corporation is the only company offering funding; nobody else wants to." He assured Fred he had talked to several of his associates in the life insurance industry, and none were interested in offering funding.

"Your actuaries need more time," Fred replied. "The customer would make a selection among mutual funds and decide what he wanted to buy. With long-term growth, mutual funds serve as collateral for a loan that pays the annual premiums on the life insurance. The funds would grow sufficiently over the customer's lifetime to pay off the loan when he dies. His family would receive the face amount of his life insurance policy and whatever mutual funds were left over. It is a step towards financial planning. Pioneer Life salesmen need it."

Sensing Forrest's impatience, Fred lit another cigarette.

"Sorry," Forrest said. "Financial Planning is off the table. One, we don't sell mutual funds. Two, if we wanted to have a second field force of registered representatives, we would have to create a broker-dealer to service them or put together a deal with someone who already has a broker-dealer. Three, we need our attorneys to handle the state insurance commissioners. And four, I don't need another set of lawyers in Washington."

Disappointment swept through Fred. He gripped the armrest on his chair and scooted forward. *Why was Forrest ignoring the effort I put into this proposal?* Fred thought. He wasn't ready to drop the subject.

"I'm offering you our General Agent position on the West Coast," Forrest exhaled a puff of smoke. "The company wants to develop a sales force out West, and the board is prepared to start with the biggest market, California. You're the perfect man for the job. Interested?"

Where is this coming from? Fred wondered. He was glad to get the offer, but California? "That's quite an honor. I *have* recruited a few agents in my day. Being your General Agent would be a big jump in responsibility at Pioneer Life. But I'm used to tending to my business and sending one or two agents your way from time to time."

"We want to get into California, Fred. It's a huge market. I know you're tied to Pensacola." Forrest emptied his ashtray into the trash and took a sip of coffee. "Besides a nice base salary, you'll have overwrite income from policies sold by the agents you recruit. We'll cover the moving expenses for you and your family—even pay the cost of shipping your yacht to California."

"Hmm. Interesting. A real challenge." Fred flicked ashes into the ashtray. "I'll talk it over with Peggy."

"You'll still be your own boss in California Fred, and the company will provide a new office for you on Market Street in San Francisco."

The two men discussed the new life insurance position for the next forty-five minutes. Fred then stood, offered his hand to Forrest, and returned to his car. He sat at the steering wheel and wondered what this offer would get him into. He started the car and headed home.

Once at the house, Fred took Peggy's hand and kissed her on the lips. He heard the children playing hide and seek in the family room. One of the neighborhood children ran past them and into the kitchen. A board game was spread across the dining room table. Furniture had been moved to make a fort where two of the kids hid.

Jesus, is there no place for a calm conversation? Fred loved his kids but often wished they would either stay confined to one room or play outside. Peggy always argued that a home should be filled with children's laughter. She didn't seem to mind the children commandeering all the rooms.

Fred moved a pile of Tinker Toys from the living room sofa to the floor, sat down, and motioned for Peggy to join him.

She smiled, took her seat, and placed a cushion behind her back.

"You're not gonna believe this, sweetheart. Forrest made me an incredible offer today."

The noise from the children's activities heightened, and Fred felt a rise of frustration push through him. "When are those children going to stop acting like kids? Can't you quiet them down a little?" An edge lined his words.

Peggy told the children to set up their hoops and play croquet in the backyard. Returning to the couch, she gave Fred a peck on the cheek and wiped the lipstick smudge from his face.

"Mission accomplished," she said, sitting down and crossing one leg over the other.

"Forrest wants me to be his General Agent. I'd recruit life insurance agents for Pioneer Life on the West Coast."

Thunder rumbled in the distance, and Peggy's brow wrinkled. "Congratulations, my love." With a quizzical eye, she crossed her arms against her chest and sat without saying a word.

"But what?" Fred asked.

"No 'but' dear. It's just that I wonder about the children. The summer's coming, and Bruce is excited about his first year in high school in the fall."

Fred stroked his chin, then smiled. "Hold on; I only told Forrest I'd think about it."

"But you *do* want this position, right?"

Fred looked out at the dark clouds moving toward the golf course. "It would be quite a promotion. I'd oversee life insurance sales for Pioneer Life throughout the West."

"Sounds like a dream." Peggy gave a worried glance at the gathering clouds.

"Nothing like the scent of fresh rain," Fred said, leaning back against the seat cushion as he closed his eyes. "I don't think they have many thunderstorms in California."

Aware of Peggy's fear of thunder and lightning, especially with their home near the Gulf, he thought this might interest her. "And the kids can still play outside, just like here, but without the humidity."

As heavy storm clouds lumbered toward them, Peggy got up. "I should get the kids in."

**

With his mind racing, Fred had trouble getting to sleep that night. *This move would be a significant change. My dream for financial planning would be put on hold, but that's okay for now. I was only twenty-two years old when selected to be a member of the Young President's Organization. The YPO is a harbinger of running a major corporate*

conglomerate, another objective for the long haul.
This promotion could set me on my way to
corporate management—one of my long-time goals.

Conglomerates are in the news these days.
Then I would focus on financial planning. No
matter how attractive California might be, Peggy
doesn't want to move. Except for decisions about
my job, she calls the shots for this family.

In the kitchen before breakfast the next
morning, Fred took Peggy's hand, pulled her close,
and kissed her. "Forrest needs an answer, honey.
It'll take time for him to qualify a new general
agency in California. This is a big financial
commitment for Pioneer Life. Forrest has to start
making plans now. He knows my focus is financial
planning. But he wants me to concentrate on life
insurance sales. Put financial planning aside for
now. It's time for me to fish or cut bait."

He took a sip of the fresh coffee Peggy had
percolated. "I know we've enjoyed many wonderful
times here . . ."

As if waiting for a doctor's diagnosis, Fred
sat quietly. It was hard for him to read Peggy's

eyes. Although the move and the new position intrigued him, he didn't want to go forward without Peggy on board.

"You decide. I'll support whatever you choose." She smiled like a Cheshire cat. "Anyway, I know you." She winked. "We'll start planning for the move." She touched his hand with hers. "I love you."

"Are you sure you are open to this? It's important to me you are happy."

"All that matters is that I'm with you. That's what makes me happy."

A surge of excitement slammed through Fred. *I want the job. And if Forrest eventually relents, it would be a step toward funding and financial planning. Once I get to California, I'll keep the funding conversation going with Forrest. He really should give more thought to funding. In time, I'll change his mind. Get him to put his toe in the water. But first, I'll concentrate on building a new sales force to sell Pioneer life insurance in California.*

CHAPTER TWO

The Golden Gate

Fred and Peggy arranged for a flight to San Francisco, and a neighbor to care for the children while they were gone. After renting a convertible, Fred drove Peggy through San Francisco then headed for the Golden Gate Bridge. The beauty of The City awed Peggy, who wished Fred could see how the San Francisco Bay surrounded it to create such beauty. They crossed the bridge and headed for Marin County. Fred told her that Forrest had located a rental home for them in Tiburon. They were on their way to check it out.

The sizeable traditional house sat atop a hill overlooking the Corinthian Yacht Club and its marina. There was a spectacular view of ocean ships moving between the Bay and the Pacific.

Several smaller boats—both sail and motor—were headed back and forth in Raccoon Straits. It was quite a sight as one looked toward Angel Island.

Fred knew that Peggy was enamored by her surroundings. He explained that a short drive from that house would take him to his office in San Francisco.

"I think you'll love this house. And if we get comfortable here, it comes with an option to buy." Fred drove up the twisting blacktop road to the house.

Peggy said, "I can't wait to go in, but I don't know how it will work out for the children clear up here on the top of this hill. Seems like a mountain. It must be a long way from schools." She showed little enthusiasm.

Fred kept pushing. "When you want to go shopping in The City, or when we want to see a play, the Sausalito ferry boat will take us in—no hassle finding a parking place."

After viewing the house and its surroundings, Peggy's concern settled around the children. "There's no place for the kids to play."

She felt her seat belt to make sure it was still secure. "You'll have your cabin cruiser and your Jaguar convertible to enjoy, Fred. I want the kids to have a place too."

"Of course," Fred replied, as they pulled into the driveway.

"Finding the *right* place for the children and me is priority number one. Wouldn't you agree?"

"Yes dear, you are absolutely—"

"I want to be near a hospital in case we need one. And we can't wait too long to pick the right school district for the kids. *Your* business location? Sorry, Fred, that's not topping my list."

Peggy's firm tone surprised Fred—she always left the big things to him. It didn't take long for Fred to realize that the environment for the children really belonged in her domain. After they toured the potential rental, Fred agreed to look for another house. They felt Marin County was the right place—near San Rafael—and an excellent place to raise a family. But the Tiburon house would not fill the bill.

While in the area, Peggy checked school availability. She registered the family with Marin General Hospital and selected St. Raphael's Catholic Church in San Rafael for their grade school.

The morning "finger of fog" from the Pacific Ocean drifted over Marin County and San Francisco, and then into the Bay. It retreated over the Sausalito hills and the Golden Gate Bridge on its way back to the ocean in afternoons. It was a beautiful sight—one that could be enjoyed all summer long.

***

After two days in Marin County, Peggy flew back to Pensacola while Fred stayed behind to check on his office in San Francisco. Forrest had provided Fred with a temporary office at 220 Bush Street, on the tenth floor of the Bush Building near Market Street. The office was so small that Fred thought the original design must have set the room up for storage. He found a phone booth on Market Street and called Forrest.

"This office isn't much bigger than my Florida garage," Fred complained. "And it's not on Market Street."

"I know, Fred; it's the best we could do on short notice. At least you're in the financial district. I'm setting up your new office in the American Savings Building on Market Street, but it will take a while. Anyway, for the next month or so, you'll spend more time driving than sitting. That nice convertible of yours is on its way and should serve you well as you get acquainted with Northern California. You have a lot of people to meet."

"Damn it. I thought you said the office was ready." Fred didn't hide his irritation.

"Sorry, Fred. I was told it would be. The time passed us up."

***

Fred began his search for life insurance agents by introducing himself at various Life Underwriter meetings on the San Francisco Peninsula and down to San Jose. "Captive" life insurance agents were limited to selling policies issued by one life insurance company. Their corporate home office would provide them with office space, a telephone, and secretarial service.

"Independent" agents could sell life insurance contracts for various life insurance companies, but those agents mostly used one or two companies for most of their sales. The independent agents had to pay for their overhead. Fred's focus was independent agents. After a few months traveling around the North Bay, he called Forrest Senf.

"Forrest, the biggest obstacle turns out to be Equity Funding Corporation. Their agents promote funding; it's a powerful sales tool. They tell prospective customers to buy mutual funds to use as collateral for a loan that pays the premium on their life insurance policy. The loan gets paid off from the insurance policy or by selling some of the mutual funds when the insured customer dies."

"I know how it works Fred. Just *forget* your funding ideas and concentrate on recruiting. Go after the independent life insurance agents. I know it's tough competition; that's why I sent *you* out there."

"But Equity Funding must be doing something right. Reported sales soared almost as fast as Equity's common stock grows on the American Stock Exchange."

"Sorry, Fred. We're not ready to get involved with funding," Forrest said, voice firm. "I don't want to get into the credit business. Our focus is life insurance, not making loans. If you need any more help in marketing life insurance, call me at another time when we can discuss it."

Fred used periodic Life Underwriter meetings—which provided a venue to network with other agents and insurance companies—to introduce Pioneer life insurance policies, mutual fund products, and financial services to his prospects. Fred attended a meeting at the Four Flags Motel in Oakland during his first month in California. Once introduced, Fred presented a competitive ten-year term life insurance policy—underwritten by Pioneer Life—to agents. He explained the ideas, answered questions, and passed out brochures.

At the get-together following the meeting, Fred passed out his business card as he made new acquaintances. As the first year drew to an end, Fred had assembled a potent stable of life insurance agents, which pleased Forrest.

Fred soon realized he wasn't the only fisherman in the sea. He encountered fierce competition from Jim Barns, a wholesaler for West Coast Life Insurance Company. Like a hungry hawk, Jim circled the field in search of agents. He offered quality life insurance products from a good company with very competitive sales commissions.

***

After graduating from West Point, Jim Barns served as an Army paratrooper. He spent his active duty time with the 82nd Airborne Infantry at Fort Bragg, North Carolina—the largest military installation in the world. President Eisenhower wanted to keep the 82nd Airborne in strategic reserve in the event of a Russian attack. In those days, United States citizens harbored memories of Sputnik and were concerned about Russia's nuclear missiles. Some built bomb shelters in their basements or garage.

With broad shoulders and thick brown hair, Jim Barns looked like a paratrooper. His charisma drew people from all lifestyles. When he talked, it seemed he and the listener were the only two people in the room. Women were attracted to his positive attitude, masculine features, deep voice, and charming smile.

Jim had a certain way about him with life agents and investment reps. He knew the life insurance business well, and he taught them how to pursue their production objectives with good commissions. He always seemed to be more interested in listening to the person who he was speaking with than the other recruiters were. They were comfortable with Jim and always welcomed him when he called on them. A relentless recruiter, Jim led West Coast's life insurance production in California. Although he did enjoy women and professional football, Jim let no other significant "outside interests" get in his way. He mixed his business and social activities artfully.

Jim Barns decided early on he was not cut out for military retirement. When he entered West Point as a freshman, part of his reasoning was patriotic—the country was at war. From Jim's viewpoint, the situation at his home was a form of war. Constant criticism from his mother and the absence of a full-time father at home energized his search for greener pastures.

He loved the army, but after his required duty time passed, he resigned and went into life insurance. Jim quickly made friends and consulted on life and annuity products for various insurance companies. Jim focused on high commissions. He was also a key player in the mutual fund industry that Fred wanted to take on.

Following one underwriter dinner in Bakersfield, Jim Barns left the group of agents to have a drink with a blonde seated at the bar. The two soon disappeared. Fred didn't see Jim again until breakfast the next morning.

From his ranch style home in Fresno, Jim searched for agents and representatives in San Diego and the Riverside-San Bernardino metropolitan area (known as the Inland Empire). Jim and Fred would often compete for the same agents in central and northern California.

Jim was not as successful at home as he was with his business activities. He knew his wife, Mary, was unhappy. "Well, you finally decided to come home for one of Robert's games," she said as Jim came into the kitchen.

"Nice to see you again too, dear." Jim dropped his clothes bag on the floor and gave her a peck on her left cheek.

Mary didn't return the kiss. "How long will you be here *this* time? The girls, especially Sarah, have been asking me when you'd be home."

"I stopped at the local market and brought a pretty good carload of groceries. Is there some room in the freezer?"

"Thanks for that." Mary had a smile on her tired face. "I hope we can all have time with you. It's been too long." Tears formed in her eyes.

He closed the refrigerator door and draped his coat over a kitchen chair. "You know I've got to earn money to cover the household expenses. I put another thousand dollars into your checking account yesterday.

Robert, Jim's son, approached with a football in hand. "C'mon, Dad, let's toss it around in the yard." Jim and Robby headed out the door for the backyard.

"How's football going, Robby?" Jim asked. "I stayed in touch with your coach while I was away. He thinks you've got what it takes to make the team. You might even make captain next year."

Try as he might, things at home stayed rocky. An absent husband with a philandering eye had shattered Mary's dream of a warm home and a close family. When Jim was gone, Mary tried to make the best of it and spent most of her time reading and playing with the girls. But the kids were growing up fast. Jim, who was seldom home for their school and sports activities, was missing it all.

By the time Fred came into the recruiting scene, Jim had realized he needed to live in an environment free of constant arguments. He wanted a place where he didn't need excuses for the time he spent on the road. Finding a permanent apartment in California topped his to-do list.

***

Beyond the competitive spirit of both men, an affinity evolved. Fred and Jim often discussed their common enemy in the recruiting wars, Equity Funding Corporation. It was difficult for them to compete with the huge life insurance and mutual funds sales that Equity Funding continued to report. Equity's common stock kept soaring on the American Stock Exchange. The only company in the financial services industry to offer funding, Equity's fancy offices and full-time secretaries were hard to match.

"You always urge me to get into the funding business," Jim told Fred. "I told West Coast Life that funding should be a part of my consulting work, and the company should take a closer look at it. But they're not budging. I explained how funding would help me to enlist recruits. Sure, I have an edge on the competition with our high commissions, but I want funding. West Coast Life refuses to listen."

"What are you doing about it?"

"I tried to get a position with Equity Funding last year, specifically to use their funding, but they said no—they preferred to train individuals to do things their way. I tried to recruit some of their better producers for West Coast Life, but that net is dry. Their agents stay put."

"I see funding as a step," Fred said. "It could kick-start financial planning, which should be integrated with the customer's financial objectives anyway. Salesmen need to become financial advisors—teach their client how to set and implement his family goals for the long haul. Funding can be an important first step in that direction."

"Jesus, Fred, you've got to get off this financial planning idea. Only one funding company is open for funding business, and it's not Pioneer Life."

At many of his initial meetings with prospects, Fred introduced the use of financial seminars to gather potential customers. Seminars made it easier for agents to sell life insurance. Recalling his commitment to Forrest, he tried to stop talking to prospects about financial planning. Fred's recruiting bore fruit, but Jim Barns still outdistanced him. Fred decided he should knuckle down and focus on life insurance.

After one life underwriters' meeting in San Jose, Fred noticed Jim on the other side of the motel restaurant. He was engrossed in a conversation with a woman he was dining with. Fred was sure Jim's plans for the evening went well beyond dinner. After they finished their dessert, she thanked Jim with a lovely smile and left.

From a distance, Fred read the disappointment on Jim's face. Fred picked up his scotch on the rocks and headed to Jim's table. After a nod from Jim, he seated himself in the woman's empty chair.

"Hey, Jim! How's it going?"

"It was going pretty well for a while there. I wanted to show her my room; she wanted to see a movie." Jim laughed. "Sometimes, the stars refuse to line up." Jim picked up a cupcake on a plate near his coffee and offered one to Fred. "How's it going with you? What kind of reception have you been getting to your financial planning ideas?"

"That's a long way off." Fred pulled out a Marlboro and lit it. "But in this economy, the guys I'm trying to recruit would make a move if I could offer them funding. They're interested in charging fees for financial advice, but they can't see fees replacing their commissions. Financial planning doesn't need to replace commissions. It gets the customer involved in creating their financial plan instead of just buying whatever the rep wants to sell him."

"What's so special about financial planning and those fees?" Jim asked. "Commissions for selling mutual funds have worked fine for as long as I can remember. Yeah, commissions are a bit of a conflict, but that's how the system works. Without a broker, the client ends up with no stock, and the broker makes no money."

Fred grimaced. "That's not right. A commission is nothing more than a fee for every purchase or sale. An advisory fee still leaves room for smaller commissions. The agent or rep earns a fee for financial advice for the long haul. Investments and life insurance should both focus on the future. Why not be honest? Charge the customer for teaching them how to set long-term goals. The advisor would recommend affordable investments. It's not rocket science."

Fred took a sip of his scotch, and Jim glanced around the room. At the bar, a gorgeous redhead sat by herself. "Maybe we should finish this conversation tomorrow when we both can concentrate."

"Take your focus off the knockout and bring it back to me," Fred said as if he were reciting a spell.

"Seriously? You want me to choose you over that redhead?"

"Give me a couple more minutes," Fred replied.

"Okay, I'm all ears," Jim smiled.

"Okay. Financial planners. They recognize the inherent conflict," Fred said. "A few mutual fund companies are experimenting with no-load or low-load mutual funds. The salesman won't get such high commissions, but he'll earn advisor fees. These new mutual funds charge a small commission when the client buys. If he chooses to get out early and sell his funds, he will be charged a fee or a low commission when he leaves."

Jim nodded and gave a small nod to the waitress.

"What can I do for you," the waitress asked Jim.

"Could you send a drink to the lovely lady at the bar? Whatever she wants." Jim winked.

The waitressed turned and headed toward the redhead.

"So how do we keep the customer invested?" Jim asked.

"That's the objective of no-load funds. Advisory fees keep the planner's interests aligned with his client's. I know we can't jump to the finish line from the get-go, but if we don't try, we'll never get there. The goal is for the clients to build wealth and security using simple investments like mutual funds while protecting their families with life insurance."

"How are you going to convince agents and reps to change?" Jim glanced at the woman who gave him a smile and raised her glass of red wine.

"I would start with financial seminars. The agent invites potential customers to a conference room in a local motel. He supplements his invitation with newspaper and radio ads, if he wants. We could have a local attorney talk about wills and trusts—I think the attorneys would come. It would be good exposure since they're not allowed to advertise."

"Using your seminars is a good idea," Jim replied. "Educating the seminar attendees makes sense. But salesmen need cash now, not an ongoing percentage of assets under management in the future. I don't think you can make them move without commissions to motivate them."

"Being a pioneer is never easy. If neither of our life companies will go for funding, we should start our own."

"I'm not so sure I want to be a pioneer," Jim replied. "Pioneers end up with arrows in their chest.

Anyway, why are you bringing this up?" Jim stretched out in his chair to listen.

"Funding is coming," Fred said, "and we should be ready. We could do good work with funding if we put our heads together. Do you have any interest in financial planning?"

"You're talking about financial advice for fees, right?"

"Well, not just that. Financial planning has to be phased in. The financial assets of the client should dictate the advisory fee. As his mutual funds grow, so will the income of the agent. Agents will accept financial planning when they see how it benefits both the customer and themselves. We could recruit more independent agents if funding is available. They *have* to take the long view of the future, or they'll get killed in this horrendous economy."

Fred got no response. "It's been a long day, and it's getting late." Fred swallowed the rest of his scotch. "Looks like another one ahead. Give it some thought, Jim."

If Jim and I ever got on the same page, we'd make progress by starting with seminars. He's good. There's a whole new world out there, and I believe it will set commissions in the background. Financial planning is on the horizon. If we could find a company willing to learn what's coming, many agents and reps would go for it.

***

After searching Marin County from Novato to the Golden Gate Bridge, Fred located a home near the Loch Lomond Marina in San Rafael. The white ranch-style house, located on Aliseo Drive in Greenbrae, overlooked much of the east shore of San Francisco Bay. There were five bedrooms, a large grassy yard for a play area, and a generous size pool with a hot tub and diving board. A guesthouse sat off the flagstone patio, and the property was gated.

For Peggy, it was love at first sight. She gasped, and her eyes lit up. Marin General Hospital and the San Rafael Catholic Church were just over the hill that separated Greenbrae and San Rafael.

Downtown San Francisco was less than ten miles away.

"How can we afford it?" Peggy asked.

"Forrest Senf paid all of our expenses for the move, plus a generous move-in bonus. Some stock in our portfolio will help finance the property.

"You amaze me, Fred. I don't know how you keep doing it."

A broad smile lit up Fred's face. "When you want something done, give it to a Marine! I'm happy you love it too." He lifted her off her feet and spun her around. "I adore you."

***

Ralph Major lived on Bretano Drive, a street at the bottom of the hill that led to Peggy and Fred's new home. Ralph was president of United American Life Insurance Company headquartered in Novato. United American Insurance Company, a casualty insurer, was also in Novato. Both were subsidiaries of the United Express Company, the issuer of The Blue Card—*the* credit card for upscale customers. United Express has other subsidiaries, including

Boston Mutual Funds. Each subsidiary has its own independent sales force.

Both Fred and Ralph were members of the Corinthian Yacht Club in Tiburon—the second yacht club in Northern California, and one of the oldest on the West Coast. San Francisco was located across Raccoon Strait. Two islands separated the Corinthian from The City: Angel Island and Alcatraz. The Corinthian Yacht Club has been in its original location since its founding in 1886. Although Fred and Ralph were competitors in the life insurance business, they became fast friends.

***

The corporate structure of United Express enchanted Fred. *This is my first chance to get to know United Express. It could be a natural fit for financial planning. If the life insurance and mutual fund subsidiaries worked with their respective agents and reps, financial planning could be achievable. But that scenario is not on the table. United Express is one of the largest conglomerates in the country. Working by myself or with Jim could start us on a new path—with funding.*

Fred's commitment to recruiting agents for Pioneer's Life Insurance stood, but Forrest continued to shun financial planning. The actuaries at Pioneer Life told Forrest not to offer funding, but allowed Fred to promote his seminars as long as they sold life insurance. Fred saw no path to that future with Pioneer Life. He would do his job and support his family, but his dream had to stay on hold. He felt like he had one foot on the dock, the other in the water.

***

Ralph Major passed Fred's ideas on to Bill Bretton, Senior Vice President of United Express for Mergers and Acquisitions. While in San Francisco to appraise another broker-dealer, Bill told Ralph he'd like to hear more about Fred's ideas. "Invite Fred to join me at the Marines Memorial Club in The City," he told Ralph.

Fred couldn't resist. He drove to San Francisco and joined Bill Bretton for cocktails at the restaurant. Bill's interest in using seminars to attract new customers excited Fred, and he looked forward to discussing it.

"Our president, Howard Roberts, has been thinking about using seminars to attract new credit card users in the Midwest. When I told him about your plan to use financial seminars to attract life insurance customers, he thought it could make sense for United Express. What's your take on using seminars to augment the United Express credit card base?

Fred couldn't sit still. *If Mr. Roberts' thinking is that refined, joint seminars could have two goals: expanding his credit card base for them, and financial planning for us.* Fred pulled a Cross pen from his shirt pocket and made several diagrams on the back of his cocktail napkin. He explained how their life insurance and mutual fund subsidiaries could work together to create financial planning as a new investment opportunity in the financial services industry.

"That makes sense," Bill replied. "But merging the cultures of our life insurance and mutual fund subsidiaries is easier said than done.

We've also been looking at ways to introduce no-load mutual funds. The broker-dealer I'm meeting with on this trip uses no-load funds. Your financial planning concept could make sense."

Delighted with Bill's initial response, Fred wouldn't let it drop. "Bill, it would take strong direction from the top and a lot of coordination. Each subsidiary focuses on its business plan. They'd have to look at the broad objectives. United Express is a conglomerate. The parts have to coordinate their activities for the benefit of the whole. If they can't see it, we must tell them. That can only come from the top."

"I'll bring it up next time I get together with Howard. Let's keep in touch." They shook hands and exchanged business cards.

Fred returned to his San Francisco office. *I won't tell Jim about this meeting right now—he's still focused on his life insurance production. We both want to introduce funding to make it easier to get recruits. United Express could provide us with the platform we need for full financial planning, but*

Jim's not on board yet. I'll also try to keep future relationships open.

CHAPTER THREE
A Chance Encounter

In June 1971, Rick Taylor spent two weeks on active duty with his Navy reserve squadron VA 731 for annual reserve duty near Reno, Nevada. The squadron went to work dropping practice bombs in the Nevada desert from their A-1 'Spad' dive bombers. Following the refresher exercises, Rick climbed aboard his old Navy Spad and headed home. He was eager to hold Peggy in his arms again—two weeks is a long time. The national weather report forecast extreme weather for the northern route back to Michigan through the plains states. Rick decided to fly the southern route instead. He took off for El Paso where he could refuel for the long flight going east across Texas.

Rick flew his plane south and east to approach the El Paso airport. Riding the bumpy air with all the punches the storm could throw at him, Rick did his best to control the plane. He glanced at the flight instruments. *It would take a monster storm to break up this old Spad.*

With no visibility in the clouds, he depended on his flight instruments to guide him. Violent up-and-down drafts made it difficult to hold a steady course. He pulled back on the throttle to slow the plan, as it descended.

Damn! Maybe I should have stayed on my original plan through the middle of the country. It couldn't get much worse than this. He keyed his microphone and called flight service for a weather update. They told him that things had deteriorated, as a massive sand storm moved toward the field.

After a bumpy approach and a problematic landing, Rick had the plane refueled, made sure his aircraft was secure for the night and stopped at the airport restaurant for a bite to eat. He hoped this beast of a sandstorm would blow itself out by morning.

As he left the restaurant, he heard a jet approaching the field. He couldn't see the plane through the dark, menacing clouds. *God, I'm glad to be on the ground,* Fred thought. He climbed the motel stairs and unlocked his room. After draping his flight jacket over a chair, he put his aerial navigation gear on the bed, plunked into a chair, and took a slow breath.

The wind continued to howl. Traces of red sand blew into his room at the windowsill and under the door. *I've never seen anything like this. God, I hope my old Spad can survive. Should have put her in a hangar rather than tying her down on the ramp. I'll have the mechanic check the plane for sand before I take off in the morning.*

A knock on the door brought him out of his thoughts. "Yeah?" he called. Another knock. Rick opened the door. "Holy shit! Fred Maloney, what the hell are you doing here?" he gasped.

Fred stepped into the room with a big smile on his suntanned face. He dropped his aviation charts and flight gear on the bed and shook hands with Rick. They patted each other on the back and broke into laughter. Rick noted that Fred wore the insignia of a Marine major on his flight suit.

"Same as you, old buddy—looking for a bed," Fred said. "I was on my way back to the Alameda Naval Air Station from New Orleans, the sky darkened. My radio announced an imminent sandstorm. Deciding to land and wait it out, I closed my flight plan. The sandstorm reached the field at the same time as me. It wasn't too bad at thirty thousand feet, but on the way down, the ride was rough. A vicious crosswind compromised my landing runway, but I managed to land the ole gal.

Once on the ground, I spotted an ancient dive bomber. I taxied my A-4 Skyhawk to a tie-down slot and then asked the lineman who was flying the A-1 Skyraider. He mentioned your name and said you had a room for the night."

"You've got to be kidding! How long has it been Fred—three, four years?"

"I don't know, but a lot of time has passed. That's for damn sure." Fred reached into the pocket of his flight suit sleeve, retrieved a pack of Marlboros, and offered one to Rick.

"Thanks." Rick smiled and leaned in for a light.

Rick found an ashtray and pulled another chair up to the small table. They hadn't seen each other since the year they graduated from Notre Dame. After opening a couple cans of Coke, the men relaxed.

"I think the last time I saw you was in 1958, at my wedding in Iowa," Fred recalled.

"Peggy must still be the prettiest girl in town. I never did figure out how you managed to nab her." Rick laughed. "Remember the old days when we used to sail on the Rascal?"

"I'll never forget 'em. Remember Peter 'Plop?'" Fred made a puckered face.

Rick took a swig of his coke. "Yeah. He was in charge of preparing sandwiches for our sail—to him a sandwich was plopping a huge mound of peanut butter onto each slice of bread, putting the two sides together, and flattening them. Thank goodness we had Hamms beer to help us wash down those lumps of peanut butter. After that, we had my mom make our sandwiches ahead of time."

"We always stopped at your house after a day of sailing," Fred added. "Your mom always had a warm meal ready. After dinner, your dad talked about his old sailing days on a 135-foot lumber schooner on Lake Michigan that sailed between Green Bay and Chicago. That ship brought northern lumber down from Muskegon to Chicago. Your Dad said that before his time, the ship had been used to haul lumber to rebuild after the great Chicago fire."

"That's right!" Rick slapped his knee. Remember the time we rented that old Aeronca from Doc Bittle on his little grass field in Mishawaka? The engine didn't meet flight standards, so we taxied back to the office. To prove the plane was okay, Doc got in and took off. At about four hundred feet in the air, the engine started sputtering."

"But he did get it back to the field without hitting any trees," Fred piped in. "That was toward the end of our college days. You had just finished your four years of active duty as a Navy pilot, and I was on my way to Pensacola to become a Marine pilot."

"I can't believe how long it's been." Rick tipped off the ashes into the ashtray. "I've spent the last few years practicing law in Detroit. Like many of us in the southeastern Michigan winter, I've had an eye on California. But we're pretty comfortable there now. Gloria likes being near Ann Arbor where she has lots of friends with children in the same schools as ours. It's a good job. My focus is on corporate and securities law and labor relations. God, Fred, where did the time go?"

"I don't know. Seems like it was only yesterday when we were in college." Fred stood up and moved around the small room. A tear balance in the corner of his eye. "It's a small world, all right. I live in the San Francisco Bay Area now. Didn't think I would ever leave Pensacola. My boss at Pioneer Life made me an offer I couldn't refuse. That was enough to get me into the management game. I'm now his General Agent on the West Coast.

"Peggy and I still look forward to your Christmas cards every year." Fred wiped his eyes, took a slug of coke, and flopped back into a chair.

"If you ever have thoughts about bringing your family to California, think about the Bay Area, Fred. Even in this lousy economy, it's a dynamic environment—plenty of opportunities. I've been recruiting and training life insurance agents in the Bay Area for Pioneer Life from my office in San Francisco."

"Really. What are your plans?"

"There's another opportunity on the horizon I'm excited about." Fred reached for another cigarette. "My buddy, Jim Barns, is a West Point Academy grad. He served in Nam as a paratrooper but decided he wasn't cut out for military retirement. He's not a pilot, but he's spent plenty of time in the air.

"Investments, especially the use of leverage in investments, fascinate Jim. He got a Master's from MIT while figuring out what he wanted to do. He eventually settled on life insurance. We compete for life insurance agents in California."

Fred inhaled his cigarette and then blew out smoke rings. He offered the pack to Rick, who shook his head "no."

"Jim's a tall, good-looking guy with a presence that few can match. Agents enjoy talking with him. Women are crazy for him. You can hear his booming voice from anywhere in the room. I want to start up a new company with him. We would be a team that's hard to beat."

"Wow. What brought you two together?" Rick took another gulp of Coke.

Fred edged his chair closer to the table. "We haven't put anything together yet. We've been competing up and down the state, and we're finally talking about common goals. If we got together and did funding, we would set up a new marketing company. There wouldn't be a problem with mutual funds since we both wholesale for Boston mutual funds. But my real goal is to offer financial planning. Jim's not on board with that yet. He still wants to stay with straight life insurance and mutual funds; and he's good at it. But he's starting to think about financial planning."

"A Marine pilot and a paratrooper. Sounds interesting."

Fred smiled. "Jim is still focused on commissions. He needs nudging if he's ever going to sell financial planning to independent agents and reps."

"That's a lot on your plate," Rick said. "But I think you're right about financial planning. It could be the best financial service in the future. People have gotten used to buying whatever the salesman pushes. Nothing fuels a strong case of malaise like a sputtering economy. People need to decide what's best for themselves. Not everyone can afford to go to a lawyer for that kind of advice. They need help them from someone who's not just pushing product."

Rick could hear the wind moan and wondered if it was an omen.

"Rick, you're right on! If you ever decide to move to California, keep me in mind. If Jim and I do put something together, maybe you can help us make it work. We could use a good attorney. And, I can help you find your way around the Bay."

The men continued talking and got to bed close to midnight.

By the next day, the storm had blown itself out, but clouds remained dark and thick. Rick filed an instrument flight plan to Dallas, where he planned to stop and refuel on the way home. He climbed to 13,000 feet and leveled off. His big radial engine purred nicely. The AD-1 performed well. He set his heading, engaged the autopilot, and reflected on his serendipitous visit with Fred.

My active duty as an aircraft carrier pilot showed me that the young pilots and bombardiers prepared for any challenges and always handled it well. I knew I should keep in touch with some of them in case I wanted to start a business—but I didn't. I wonder if this new idea of Fred's will gain any traction. He's been on a mission for the last few years. If he gets it off the ground, I could help him get some altitude. He'll be facing some legal problems and will need a good attorney.

When Rick Taylor returned to his Detroit law office, his desk cried for attention. He opened the top file and went to work. But his mind kept drifting back to El Paso. He thought about his place in the Detroit law firm. Second-generation family members ran the firm—some had sons also practicing law there. He knew his financial future had its limits. The senior partners, who were well-connected in the community, brought in most of the new business.

In the years he had spent with the law firm, Rick made little time for politics in Detroit. Since graduation from Michigan Law School, his firm had treated him well. Two of the partners had sons who were Michigan law grads. One son, Pat, specialized in plaintiff litigation. He and Rick got along well.

I've brought several lucrative plaintiff cases to the firm over the past few years, and the firm allowed me to share fees in the judgments I secured.

The other son, Grafton, was focused on labor law. There were no contingent fees in that field, but the income to the firm from that practice was steady. With so many family members involved, partnership in the law firm was a distant goal. Rick wanted to explore opportunities. He kept an eye on *The Wall Street Journal*.

Rick glanced at the file he'd just opened. *Darn, another litigation defense case. I'd rather have a few plaintiff cases of my own. The time frame involved in defense cases says little for justice. You keep giving reports to the insurance companies.*

How could Fred give up the comfortable life he had in Pensacola? Probably because he's passionate about having a new mission.

***

Gloria Taylor found life in Pittsfield Village, near the Ann Arbor campus of the University of Michigan Law School, much to her liking. When the Maloneys first moved there, Rick was still in law school. Many newlyweds lived in the village— some studying at the University of Michigan and some working in nearby communities to support themselves while waiting to attend the university. It was only a short drive from Pittsfield Village to the Detroit law office where Rick Taylor began his long-desired legal career. Rick focused on corporate, securities, and labor law. With all its manufacturing facilities and unions, the Detroit area had fertile fields.

Rick had met Gloria at a pep rally the night before a Michigan football game. Michigan would host Indiana the next day. Rick wore a red Borsalino wide-brimmed felt hat with a long, pointed sunscreen he'd bought in Italy. As he moved around the dance floor, all the girls wanted to touch the hat. Gloria ended up with the hat, and Rick ended up with Gloria.

After nine years of marriage, Gloria knew that Rick hadn't found his legal niche yet. Rick seemed enthused after a weekend of flying with the Naval Reserves, but he didn't talk much about the office when he came home from work.

Rick and Gloria played cards after supper when they weren't going out. One evening, to his surprise, Rick found Gloria lounged on the living room couch, watching TV. She had placed one of his favorites, a Manhattan, alongside her cocktail on the alligator tray in the center of the coffee table. Gloria, beautiful in her blue silk nightgown, had a hint of a smile on her lips and a twinkle in her eye.

Gloria always seemed to get it—she had that Midwestern common sense when it came to emotions. From the tone of his voice on the phone earlier that day, Gloria thought she knew what Rick would want to talk about. Gloria's steady glance warmed Rick as they sat on the couch.

"I know that you've always had a gleam in your eye for California. All you've talked about since El Paso is the energy you felt while you and Fred were together. I know we've talked about buying a house here in Ann Arbor, but I can feel those California strings tugging at your heart." Gloria took a sip of her drink.

Rick smiled and took his seat on the couch. He smoothed out the decorative pillow, gave Peggy a big kiss on the lips, and stroked her brown hair. They enjoyed a long, warm conversation before heading to bed.

The next week, Rick responded to a *Wall Street Journal* solicitation for a labor relations attorney in San Francisco. It was a good job but not with a law firm. The Distributors Association represented warehouse owners on the San Francisco and Oakland docks. Rick would draft documents and administer and negotiate labor contracts with

Jimmy Hoffa's Teamsters and Harry Bridges' International Longshore and Warehousemen's Union.

"But I thought you were more interested in getting into plaintiff litigation. I know you've been negotiating contracts with the Detroit auto unions, but these people are looking for someone to handle labor relations on the docks," Gloria said.

"Well, that's part of it. They know my preference, but think I will be a good fit for the job anyway. I can do it while I study for the California Bar Exam. There's usually a delay of several months from taking the exam to getting the results and finding a job. They told me they also need lawyers."

Fred and Gloria talked it over for the rest of the evening, and then again, the next day. Gloria felt it was time to move on from Pittsfield Village.

"You know what kind of law practice you want, Rick. That's your decision." They both agreed that the West had always been about living a dream.

***

The Taylors followed the sun and pulled a U-Haul Trailer behind their two-year-old Plymouth station wagon. As they left the Detroit city limits behind, radio station WJR announced that twenty-three inches of snow had blanketed Detroit, and trucks had spread twenty-three inches of salt on the streets. Rick and Gloria smiled as they avoided cars covered with fresh layers of soft, white snow.

Once out of Detroit, thoughts of sunshine and beaches came to everyone's mind. Gloria felt a twinge of sadness as she tried to make herself comfortable in the front seat of the station wagon. The girls were in the back with plenty of room for fun and games.

Gloria recalled memories of camping with the family in the summer and helping the girls learn to ice skate in beautiful southeastern Michigan. The family always loved travel. They even talked about buying an *Airstream* trailer after they settled in California. Rick told Gloria that the designer of that trailer also worked on the *Spirit of St. Louis*, the plane that Charles Lindberg flew solo across the Atlantic in 1927.

Gloria had always given Rick time to enjoy his small sailboat when they vacationed at a lake near Ann Arbor.

"You were always very generous, sweetheart," Rick said. "Dad introduced me to sailing when I was eleven. We went to Magician Lake where he rented a cottage for his two-week vacation from Bendix. A rowboat came with the cottage, and Dad got permission from the owner to make a sailboat out of that broken-down boat. 'As long as I can still fish with it when you finish,' he was told.

"Dad bought a couple of two-by-fours for the mast and boom, sheets of plywood, and wire cable to hold the mast vertical. From plywood, we made a rudder and two leeboards, one for each side of the boat, to keep the sailboat from being blown sideways when tacking into the wind."

"The girls cut the two sails from old bedsheets—the mainsail and jib sail. My mom sewed." Rick watched a bug slam against the windshield. "We had the only sailboat on that small inland lake. Our new friends at Magician Lake often asked if they could go for a ride, but Dad didn't want to take the chance of one of them falling off the boat. It often sailed quite a distance from the shore."

Rick turned on the wipers and washed the windshield. The car remained quiet a moment, and then Rick said, "The lust for sailing never left me. We didn't have a homemade sailboat in Michigan, but the girls always checked out the sailboats before they started looking at the other pleasure craft on the lake."

The children talked about family vacations as the station wagon rumbled toward California. They played with their dolls and toys in the back. When they became bored, Gloria played games with them: license plates, signs, and car colors.

The drive was difficult for Gloria. Pregnant with her fourth child, she felt uncomfortable most of the way. When the family stopped at the Grand Canyon, Gloria pleaded with Rick. "Yes, it's beautiful. But I don't want to get out of the car and walk around. Take the girls for a side trip and then let's get moving." She felt confined, hot, tired, and cranky.

"Honey, I wish there was something I could do," Rick said as they crossed into Nevada. "A few more mountains and we'll be in the San Joaquin Valley—then on to our new home in San Rafael. I'll find a place where we can stop for lunch and a restroom break."

Not great—but it was the best he could do.

When the Taylor family arrived in the Bay Area, they moved into their new home in the Terra Linda neighborhood of San Rafael. Rick had rented a three-bedroom Eichler in a valley surrounded by large green hills. Mount Tamalpais stood in the background. The houses, constructed of plywood siding, had enclosed garages but no attics or basements. Sand and tar topped the flat roofs. Four-by-eight sheets of plywood fencing surrounded the backyard, duplicating the adjacent Eichler on the next street. It delighted Gloria to put both feet on the ground again.

Rick assured Gloria, "Becky and Jody can have one bedroom. Susan can share the third one with the new baby. Oh, I met a nice family next door. They have a daughter about Becky's age."

Not used to living near black families, Gloria asked, "Are you sure we will be safe?"

"The Detroit riots are long gone, Gloria. Mixed neighborhoods are common in California. The realtor told me that our new neighbor is a doctor at the Marin General Hospital."

***

As Gloria became acquainted with the family next door, her fears lifted. She became good friends with neighbors on both sides. Other friends came through introductions and bridge parties. Peggy and Gloria met through their husbands. Peggy referred Gloria to a gynecologist at Marin General Hospital, and Gloria discovered she was carrying twins.

"What? Twins! No, I'm not going to have twins," she told the doctor in a loud voice.

The doctor handed Gloria her x-ray. "See, Mrs. Taylor—two spines."

"Why didn't you tell me this when I could still get my leg over the bridge rail?" she replied, stunned.

Fraternal twins, Rick and Randy, had different birthdays. One had been born just before midnight and one after. Both boys were healthy, but Randy, being a little underweight, remained at Marin General Hospital for two extra days.

***

Rick went to work on the docks in San Francisco administering labor contracts with the ILWU and the Teamsters unions. Jimmy Hoffa's Teamsters coordinated with Harry Bridges' International Longshore and Warehousemen's Union to unload ships and haul the cargo to U.S. destinations. Ray Samuels managed the Distributors Association.

San Francisco has always been a drinking town. Ray Samuels insisted that negotiations with the ILWU be in the afternoons when booze flowed freely. Distributors Association representatives were not allowed to drink alcohol at lunch.

Ray took Rick to an upcoming negotiating session with the Longshoremen at Fisherman's Wharf. When they walked in, Rick sensed tension. Immediately, the doors locked behind them and stayed that way until local Teamsters boss, Rudy Tham, ended the meeting.

Ray Samuels introduced Rick to the men, and a loud chorus of laughter came from the ranks. Rick took his seat alongside Ray and didn't mention the laughter until after the meeting.

"Rick, there's an old saying on the docks. When a longshoreman finds his way behind a shipping container to sip his bottle of bourbon, and somebody asks, 'Where's so and so,' the answer is likely to be, 'He's having a Rick Taylor.'"

Rick smiled. *Live and learn.*

When Rick told Gloria about it that night, the look in her eyes said she wondered whether they had made the right move. Rick laughed. "The pay is higher than I'd receive as a lawyer with no California law license. It'll keep me bringing in money until the bar exam results come—but I'd rather practice law.

"Ever since I was a kid, I've wanted a job I'd never have to retire from. I had no interest in working for a gold watch, a party, and retirement pay like Uncle Frank and my dad did. Uncle

Clarence had his own shoe business in Kokomo. As far as I'm concerned, working for myself and my family is a better way to go than a factory job."

"Hey, Rick," Fred said when Rick picked up the phone. "I heard about the twins. It must be tough for you to find a place to study at home." Fred laughed. "My cabin cruiser is docked at the Loch Lomond Marina over on San Pedro Road, near your house. Why don't you use the boat as a library, and you can study for your bar exam in peace?"

"That's very generous of you. I'd be close enough to home in the evenings that Gloria would feel safe being alone with the kids. If I studied at night, that wouldn't interfere with your use of the boat during the day." Then, with a chuckle, Rick said, "I know it's not a sailboat, but being tied to a dock should keep it pretty steady. Thanks for the generous offer."

After he passed the bar, Rick answered an ad in the *San Francisco Recorder* placed by Woodford and Hoskins, a law firm in the Alcoa Building near the Embarcadero. It was an old firm with deep ties in the Bay Area. Jack Woodford, a Palo Alto native, belonged to several business and social clubs on the Peninsula. Jim Hoskins, born and raised in Alameda, worked as an adjunct professor of law at Boalt Hall in Berkeley.

***

Rick walked into the offices of Woodford and Hoskins and handed his resume to the receptionist.

"Thank you," she said and headed into Mr. Woodford's office with the papers. She returned to the reception area and asked, "Can you come in tomorrow at 11:00 for an interview?"

"Yes, of course."

Rick returned the next day. Again, the secretary reported that Mr. Woodford was too busy to meet. "Can you come back tomorrow at the same time?"

The next day, the secretary asked, "Could you possibly come back at 1:30?" A hint of embarrassment lined her words.

After lunch, Rick returned to another long wait. Tired of this game, he pulled a sheet of paper from his leather briefcase and scribbled some words. Rick approached the receptionist and handed her the folded note. "Please put this on Mr. Woodford's desk."

The note said: If you are this busy, you need my help.

Minutes later, Mr. Woodford stepped through his door, left hand extended. "Would you please join me, Mr. Taylor?"

An hour and twenty minutes later, Rick left Mr. Woodford as the newest attorney with Woodford and Hoskins

On Monday morning at eight o'clock, Rick returned to the law office. He said a cheerful "good morning" to the receptionist and proceeded to Jim Hoskins' office. Mr. Hoskins introduced Rick to the other attorneys, the secretaries, and escorted Rick to his new office.

Rick paused at the classic leather-trimmed desk across from the door and admired his new office. Two overstuffed leather chairs faced the desk. Books filled the mahogany shelves that lined the wall. His view through the floor-to-ceiling windows swept eastward over Fisherman's Wharf, past Alcatraz Island, and along the Bay Bridge. Ready to realize his dream, Rick glanced at the wharves where he'd spent the last few months. *God, it's nice to be practicing law*! Letting a broad smile cross his face, he went to work arranging his new desk.

ACT II
Making it Work

CHAPTER FOUR

Get It Together

Fred didn't give up on his desire to bring funding to Pioneer Life Insurance Company, but he knew he had several other tasks. If he could get funding, he'd need Jim Barns on board. Next came the creation of a business structure to market life insurance policies that offered funding along with legal help. Fred wanted Rick Taylor on board but knew Rick wouldn't leave Hoskins and Woodford. However, Rick had offered to provide legal assistance when needed—so Fred saw no harm in asking. And last, get Marco Flynn to secure start-up money.

Now situated in his Paradise Life office in the American Savings building on Market Street, Fred hung his suit coat on the clothes rack, lit a Marlboro, and told his secretary to hold his calls.

Thoughts spun in his mind. He didn't have a corporation nor a board of directors to guide him as he proceeded on his quest, and he knew he couldn't handle the helm alone. Certain that Jim wanted to offer funding, Fred knew Jim hadn't given his wholehearted support to Fred's financial planning ideas.

Fred viewed the hazards ahead. Like a boat in shallow water, he didn't want to let his keel get stuck in the mud. He decided to create an advisory committee. Fred knew his friends would help, but they lived all around the country. Fred's first call was to Keith Raab. Keith, an Air Force general, had recently retired from the Strategic Air Command. They'd first met at the Naval Air Training Command in Pensacola back in the early sixties where they both enjoyed watching the Navy's Blue Angels aerobatic team practice their maneuvers.

Frank Gavin, another friend, owned a life insurance company in Nashville and a bank in Switzerland. Fred's relationship with Frank had evolved over the years. Frank was retired but would never admit it. He and his wife Martha were a classic example of a traditional southern couple enjoying a stately mansion in Nashville in later life.

Pat Raab was a businessman. In his youth, he moved from Canada to Marin County and went on to develop a small paper cup company. He later turned that company into a national retailer. When Fred and Keith played golf in Mobile, Pat would often join them at the Magnolia Grove Golf Club. He later became an officer of the Wells Fargo Bank.

Fred surveyed his new advisory committee about encouraging Jim Barns' interest in funding. The consensus was that working with Fred's competitor was like sailing into dangerous waters. They all agreed that Forrest Senf would not take it kindly.

Not one to give up easily, Fred thought, *If I can get funding at Pioneer Life, I'll recruit Jim Barns and perhaps he'll move his license to Pioneer Life Insurance Company.*

Fred laid his cards on the table with Jim Barns. Would he get involved in starting up a new company? Both men recruited well, but according to the financial reports filed with the California

Insurance Commissioner, Equity Funding Corporation was "eating their lunch."

It was late in the day. The San Jose Life Underwriter meeting had just concluded. Fred found Jim in the lounge as a potential recruit at Jim's table stood to leave. Fred took the empty chair.

"Hey, Jim. What are you up to? Are you staying overnight or moving on?" Fred motioned to the cocktail waitress and turned to Jim. "I've got a few things I'd like to discuss."

"I'm staying the night and heading out in the morning. What's on your mind?"

"Equity Funding is killing us, Jim, and funding is the ax they wield. I still don't know how they do it. Office to office, we are selling more life insurance than they are. Their insurance policies are no better than ours, but they've got the funding edge. Their California branches don't have many aggressive salesmen. Aggressive salesmen—ha! That's an oxymoron at Equity Funding." Fred laughed, and Jim smiled. "They rest in their luxurious offices with their telephones, the company takes care of their office expenses. What I don't get is that they keep reporting more and more life insurance sales, and the price of their common stock keeps on rising on the American Stock Exchange."

"What are you going to do about it?" Jim pulled a pack of Lucky Strikes and offered one to Fred.

Fred shook his head, retrieved his Marlboros, and said, "I'm going to figure out a way to get Forrest to offer funding—at least in a few of his policies—even if it's only a token number."

"Good luck," Jim responded with a cynical smile.

"I'm serious." Fred's eyes turned stern. He took Jim's attitude as a challenge.

Jim arched his eyebrow and looked back at Fred. "You're outta your mind. How do you think you'll make that happen?"

"I've got ideas, Jim. If Forrest agrees to try funding out, would you consider working with me—even if it means leaving West Coast Life?"

Jim Barns squirmed, scratched his chin, and looked into Fred's eyes. "You mean you want me to give up what I've got and cast my life with your dream?"

"No. But if I get Forrest to provide funding, we could put our recruiting talents together and start a new company to market funding."

"That's a great idea, Fred. But I'll believe it when I see it. Let's see some action."

***

Equity Funding Corporation is going wild with their damn funding, Fred thought as the elevator took him to his tenth-floor office in the American Savings building. *The United Express Company could provide us with funding and with financial planning, but at this point, that's not realistic. My only alternative is to get Forrest to change his mind. Frank Gavin's insurance company might hold the key to gaining momentum with Forrest. Without results, Jim won't wait around forever. Several years ago, Forrest advised Fred to: go from step A to step B, then on to step C—don't get ahead of yourself.*

Step A: Get Pioneer Life to add funding to some of its policies. For that, I need legal help—contact Rick. Step B: Jim and I start our own company. To do that right, we'll need money. Find investors. Step C: Lead the charge to challenge the financial services industry.

What the hell am I doing? I've got five kids to feed, clothe, and educate. I know Peggy. She'll humor me, but her patience won't hold on forever. The money issue for the kids, I can handle, but I have to know when I am going too far.

Thumbing through his Rolodex, Fred made notes about prospective connections. His secretary interrupted with a call from Forrest Senf.

After the usual pleasantries, Forrest said he'd be in the Bay Area the following week. "Fred, I've had phone calls from some of your new agents complaining they want more life insurance training. They say there's too much talk about financial planning."

Fred felt immediate frustration. His hands were already full, and he didn't want to get into another discussion with Forrest about the virtues of financial planning. It was time to take action. As the conversation ended, he slammed his notebook down on his desktop and crushed his half-smoked cigarette into the ashtray. He didn't want to get another lecture from Forrest.

If I'm not careful, he'll get someone else to be his General Agent in California. I've done a good job recruiting, but I need to know whether Jim and I have a realistic chance to work together. Damn it! If it isn't one thing, it's another. I don't need this right now.

There aren't enough hours in the day. I'm slacking off on my training cycle for new agents. The chance to get Jim to make a move depends on funding. Marco Flynn will help me find money, and I'll need good legal help to get that funding—Rick Taylor? He's always been there for me when I've needed help. Fred took another sip of his now cold coffee, pulled out a Marlboro, and asked his secretary to get Rick Taylor on the phone.

"Rick. I understand that you're happy over there with Hoskins & Woodford at the Alcoa Building."

"Yeah, Fred, everything's going well here. Hope things are good with you."

"I haven't seen you since you joined the law firm. Have you got time for lunch today? The Tadich Grill has a sumptuous fresh fish luncheon at noon. It's an interesting place—they've been serving excellent food since they filled in the shoreline to make room for California Street."

"Sounds great. I'd love to get caught up. See you at Tadich's at 12:15."

***

Fred selected a corner booth away from the crowd and ordered a bottle of Napa Sauvignon Blanc for the two of them. Fred saw Rick and waved him over. "Good to see you again, Rick. I hear things are going well for you at the office. How's the family? How do you like the new house?" Fred motioned to Rick to have a seat.

"Everything is great," Rick replied. "And again, thanks for letting me use your yacht to study for the bar. What a difference it made to study in silence!"

"Glad I could help."

Rick took a sip of his chilled wine and lit a cigarette. Fred ordered the local abalone for them, and they reminisced while waiting for their food. During a scrumptious meal, Fred got down to business.

"Let me run something by you. Forrest Senf will be in town next Wednesday. He wants me to stop talking about financial planning on the recruiting trail. I agreed to stop."

"That must be a tough one for you."

"Not really. Financial planning will have to wait. Jim Barns and I are considering working together, but we need funding. Forrest avoids funding—he's nervous about the liability issue; his actuaries fear premium loans; and no insurance company other than Equity Funding Corporation offers funding, nor do any plan to. Forrest has no interest in funding. His friends are suspicious of Equity Funding Corporation and say it is hard to interpret the numbers in Equity's financial reports."

"Yes, I remember you telling me about that."

"Is there anyone in your firm that works on reinsurance?"

"Sure. Jack has a few insurance clients, and he's drafted several reinsurance agreements. Why?"

"I think the liability that concerns Forrest could be insured with a reinsurance treaty or a reinsurance agreement with another insurance company."

"Yes, we've had experience with reinsurance agreements. I've researched them when I helped Jack. What are you thinking?"

"Let's say Pioneer Life Insurance Company bought reinsurance from Frank Gavin's Nashville Life Insurance Company. Could that reinsurance include funding relief for Pioneer Life? Could they transfer part of the risk involved with the repayment of the premium financing loan over to Nashville Life? That would get that risk off from Pioneer's books." Fred glanced around the packed restaurant, nodded at their menus, and after a quick scan, the men ordered calamari.

"Jack Woodford and I looked at that concept in a different context about a month ago," Rick replied. "But you're right. If Pioneer Life doesn't want to insure the risk of non-repayment of the premium loans by Pioneer Life's insured customers, they could transfer the risk to another insurance company. There's got to be another insurance company willing to assume that risk for an adequate premium. A new insurance policy would be entered into—a policy between two insurance companies. One insurance company insures a specific risk that the other company does not want to assume."

"Great," Fred said. "You've got it! I need ammunition to get Forrest to offer funding. I have another insurance company in mind: Frank Gavin's Nashville Life. Can Forrest and I meet with you next Thursday morning? Forrest will be in town, and I'd like to introduce him to your office. I'll bring up the reinsurance, which will solve the funding problem for Forrest. Who knows? If we can get funding, I think I can get Jim to move to Pioneer Life."

"Okay," Rick replied. "I'll clear my schedule for Thursday and make sure that Jack Woodford is in the office and available."

***

It was the Thursday before the New Year's holiday at the Hoskins & Woodford law office. Water, coffee, and yellow note pads lay in front of each chair at the long, mahogany table. Forrest and Fred puffed on their cigarettes. Fred had given him a heads up about the subject of discussion. Expressing a great deal of reluctance, Forrest agreed to attend. At Fred's request, Rick Taylor provided an introductory briefing on the reinsurance issue. As Forrest listened, he became more interested—there was even a hint of enthusiasm in his manner.

Rick used slides to make his points during his forty-minute presentation. After Rick finished, Forrest looked at Fred. "You know that my actuaries mentioned the possibility of reinsurance when you first it brought up funding. But you were so wrapped up with your damned financial planning idea, we decided not to go further."

That's the signal I wanted. We've hooked Forrest. When Jack Woodward supports Rick's preamble in a few minutes, it will be time for me to reel him in.

Fred watched Forrest light a cigarette. "Jim Barns and I have been after the same agents the past few months," Fred said. "Equity Funding rolls right over us. According to their published financial reports, they're selling more life insurance than Jim and me together in every office where we compete. And I mean a lot more. I don't believe their numbers, but I know that their insurance sales depend on funding. Jim and I agree—with funding, the two of us could shrink that gap."

Forrest seemed impressed.

Attorney Jack Woodward stepped in. He adjusted his documents and placed them in neat piles. Dressed in a blue suit with a colorful striped necktie—the custom in the office—he took a sip from his coffee cup and then placed it back on his saucer.

"If Pioneer Life Insurance Company can get another insurance company, say Nashville Life insurance Company, to assume the funding risk, our research indicates the Securities and Exchange Commission in Washington would approve funding as a registered security for sale to the public. Your people could then proceed to get those Pioneer policies with funding cleared by the various state insurance commissioners."

As the meeting in the Alcoa Building progressed, Forrest shuffled through his notes and the memorandum that Rick Taylor had prepared. Jack assured the attendees a facultative reinsurance agreement between two life insurance companies could transfer risk from one company to the other.

A soft silence curtained the room as everyone considered the significance of Mr. Woodward's comments.

Fred stood up. A smile broke out from under his short red crew cut and high cheekbones. His gray eyes focused on Forrest. He understood the quizzical expression on Forrest's face.

"I think I can convince Frank Gavin at Nashville Life to assume the funding risk in his insurance company. He also owns a bank in Switzerland. Perhaps it can play a part in the lending portion of funding. That could shift the negative debt issues of funding from your company to his," Fred said.

"Seems like a long shot, but I've seen you pull rabbits out of hats before," Forrest replied. "I'll check it out with my actuaries when I get back to Hartford."

***

As he drove back towards the Golden Gate Bridge, Forrest considered how Fred had persuaded him that a Pioneer Life Insurance portfolio had room for funding in some of its policies. He lit a cigarette. *How the hell did Fred manipulate me? That's the way it always seemed to happen.* Forrest stopped at the toll booth, paid his toll, and turned down Lombard and toward the San Francisco airport.

Forrest watched as Fred's Pioneer Life Insurance production continued to grow and agreed that if Jim Barns transferred his insurance license to Pioneer Life, their combined production would blossom. *That would justify putting my legal team to work on the project. I'm comfortable with Fred's assurances that Jim wants funding, but I'm not going to put up with these financial planning ideas that Fred is hung up on—I don't think Jim Barns is pushing for financial planning. I'll cross that bridge when I get to it.*

***

Fred returned to his office and called his old friend Frank Gavin in Nashville. After an exchange of pleasantries, he explained to Frank the conclusions reached during the meeting at Hoskins & Woodford.

"Frank, I think Forrest is coming around on funding. Would you consider using reinsurance at Nashville Life to back up insurance policy loans for Pioneer Life Insurance Company?"

"It's an interesting thought," Frank replied. "I know what you are asking. We need to talk more about it. New Year's Eve is only a couple of days away. Why don't you and Peggy grab a flight so that y'all can visit Martha and me to celebrate the New Year?"

"That's kind of you. We would love to join you for New Year's Eve." Fred detected confidence in Frank's voice. He then phoned Jim Barns and brought him up to date.

As though he was tired of hearing Fred's pitch, Jim said, "Fred, when are you going to settle down? I'll buy your idea when I see it."

***

Fred knew Peggy would be unhappy. He'd already taken considerable family time to chase his dream of financial planning. Now, he'd have to ask her to get someone to watch the kids while they went to Nashville. Fred wasn't eager to deal with the flack he'd run into when he got home for dinner that night.

"Hello, sweetheart. How was your day?" He kissed Peggy set his briefcase on the entrance table and hugged her. "It's been a busy day, honey. Forrest is getting serious about helping us with funding."

"That's great news! And after all the fuss he made about not wanting funding. Let's go into the living room. I'll bring our drinks in."

Fred hung up his coat and took his seat on the couch. Taking a sip of his scotch and water, he prepared himself for the storm. He glanced around the living room and the kitchen. The children were nowhere to be seen.

He told Peggy about the meeting Rick had set up for Forrest at the Hoskins & Woodford law offices, and how Forrest, reluctant at first, seemed to come around as the men made their presentations.

"We need to get another insurance company involved to make my proposal work. Frank Gavin could give us that help. He is willing to discuss the details."

"That's great news!"

"He wants us to visit him in Nashville . . ."

"How fun," she replied.

"At his place on New Year's Eve."

There. He'd said it.

Peggy's face went white. "Are you out of your mind? That's clear across the country! We are spending the holidays right here with the children. They'll be out of school. We could go out for a while on New Year's Eve, but not to Tennessee."

Peggy hadn't even touched her Rob Roy. Her brow furrowed and her jaw seemed clenched. Anger skewed her beautiful face.

Fred could see he was in trouble. He took another sip of his drink. "But honey, this is important. It's a make or break situation. If Frank agrees to my proposal, we'll have funding at Pioneer Life. I think Jim Barns will move his license over to Pioneer Life, and we'll be off and running."

"I'm disappointed, Fred." Peggy wiped a tear from her left eye. "If you think it's more important that we spend New Year's Eve in Nashville than at home with our family, you'll just have to go by yourself."

"But I already accepted the invitation, honey. We have to go."

Her scowl made Fred nervous. Funding rested on her decision. "Next time, remember to ask me before you answer an invitation for both of us. I can't believe you would desert the kids on New Year's Eve!"

They talked about the trip over dinner, and Peggy finally agreed to go—with a two-day limit. They kissed, made up, and Fred promised he would never make plans again without checking with her first.

***

The Maloneys arrived in the late afternoon on New Year's Eve. Frank's chauffeur escorted them from the terminal to the Lincoln town car. With a broad smile, Frank Gavin shook hands and welcomed Fred and Peggy.

"Martha looks forward to meeting y'all. I've been telling her about you for years, Fred."

They climbed into Frank's Lincoln limo. A gentleman farmer now, Frank owned a large amount of acreage. As the town of Nashville grew, it surrounded the Gavin property.

The chauffeur gave Fred and Peggy a tour of downtown Nashville on their way to Frank's spectacular, nineteenth-century mansion in the middle of Nashville. They approached the old colonial house and entered its circular driveway, adorned with the reindeer pulling a sleigh and a

Santa sitting in an old hay wagon that served as the sleigh. Enormous pillars stood on the front of the mansion.

Frank escorted the Maloneys into the foyer. A long hallway led to a large living room on their left. It was about the same size as the dining area to their right. Fred saw the servant quarters between the trees when he glanced through a window at the end of the hallway.

Martha Gavin gave them a warm welcome as they entered the drawing room. "So nice to see you," Martha said. "I hope your flight was comfortable."

Martha escorted Fred and Peggy up the curving staircase to the large credenza and into their bedroom. Irish lace, long felt ribbons, and taffeta covered the canopy bed. A strip of felt hung from the ceiling next to the bed. If a guest wanted service, he pulled the ribbon.

This is the old South, Peggy thought. But there was more.

After chatting in the drawing room, Martha offered dinner. A pleasant fragrance lifted from the lit candelabras on the long dining room table. When the diners wanted extra food or another desired service, a servant would magically appear. He or she would nod to a particular guest and deliver the food or perform whatever service needed.

Peggy couldn't figure out how the servants knew when to come into the dining room. Although later, she discovered the secret. On the floor, a button at Martha's chair could be clicked with her foot whenever she desired service.

Frank opened his office door and led Fred in while Peggy and Martha chatted in the drawing room. Peggy hoped she could get some insight into Frank's point of view about funding, but soon realized Frank did the business, and Martha left it entirely to him.

Martha participated in the Women's Auxiliary and volunteered at the F. J. Gavin Memorial Hospital. A founder of the Grand Ole Opera, she told Peggy that her best friend, Minnie Pearl, had been trained to be an opera singer in Austria and ended up a star in Nashville.

Later in the evening, they gathered in the drawing room with the television tuned to ABC. It was a social evening with no discussion of life insurance. Holiday melodies wove throughout the room courtesy of *The Lawrence Welk Show*.

Martha shook a small silver bell, and a servant appeared with a tray balanced on his shoulder. Each person lifted a chilled flute of champagne.

"To a profitable reinsurance policy," Frank proclaimed.

All glasses raised. Peggy winked at Fred when she realized the champagne had no bubbles; it was apple juice. Lawrence Welk displayed his best, and Fred and Peggy relaxed. The New Year's Eve celebration went on for another forty-five minutes.

When Frank turned off the television, and the ladies departed, Fred found a good position on the soft leather couch, lit a cigarette, and asked, "How do you feel about this reinsurance approach with Pioneer Life to getting funding started?"

"It makes a lot of sense for Pioneer Life. It's a new market for Forrest Senf. But I've retired. I've been through enough battles for a lifetime," Frank said. "I would, however, like to see you have access to funding."

"The finish line is still a long way off. Your help will get me around another buoy, but the finish line is financial planning. We'll have enough wind to finish the race. And it will add Jim Barns to my crew. You've been a strong force on my executive committee. If Nashville Life doesn't do the job, I'll have to start all over."

"If it were anyone but you, I'd pass without considering it," Frank said. "I understand your motives. You see funding, not only as an important product for your recruiting but also as a path to introducing financial planning. I agree funding should work well, and it will give you and Jim a new tool for recruiting."

Frank got up from his chair, walked over to the fireplace, and picked up the poker. While moving the logs around, he stayed quiet. He put the poker down, turned, and looked at Fred. "I'll help."

Fred was impressed. *Relationships count. When the going gets tough, the tough get going.*

"Coming from you, Frank, that's quite a vote of confidence. I'll never forget this. Jim Barns, by the way, is one hell of a salesman. As a team, Jim and I can make Forrest happy.

"But I still have a way to go with Jim on the future of financial planning. He's still not completely sold on the concept of fees for financial advice. Life insurance and mutual funds with commissions have been his bread and butter. I hope he'll see the advantages as we proceed and buy-in on that concept for the journey ahead."

The next day, Frank and Fred watched New Year football and talked about the proposed reinsurance agreement between Pioneer Life and Nashville Life. At halftime, they discussed Fred's proposal. Fred left his rough draft with Frank who promised to review it after New Year's Day.

Martha served Fred and Peggy an authentic southern breakfast that included grits. Although the Maloneys enjoyed the genuine southern hospitality, they decided to head home. Peggy had spent a lot of time on the phone checking in on the children, everything was going well, but she wanted to be home with the kids.

The chauffeur took the Maloneys back to the airport for their flight.

***

Rick sent a final draft of the proposed reinsurance agreement to Forrest Senf. After the actuaries reviewed it, Forrest got approval from his legal department and proceeded to integrate funding into a new line of life insurance policies by the end of February. Forrest was comfortable, reinforced by the fact that the common stock of Equity Funding not only held its strength but continued to rise. *If they can make it work, we can make it work*, he thought.

***

Rick Taylor thought he had taken a big step toward a partnership in the law firm. When Forrest retained Woodford and Hoskins to represent Pioneer Life before the Securities and Exchange Commission in Washington, D.C. Jack Woodford designated Rick Taylor to get funding approved as a security. Rick booked a hotel room at the JW Marriott hotel near the SEC building in Washington, D.C. He found a part-time legal secretary to file the required documents.

CHAPTER FIVE

Setting the Sails

With SEC approval for funding in Pioneer Life insurance policies, Rick returned to American Financial. He met with Fred and Jim in the conference room in the America Savings Building to report on the hearings.

"The funding prospectus must provide details about this investment offering of securities for sale to the public and has to meet the same criteria as a stock offering; it must include the particulars of the funding business and the transactions in question. The reinsurance documents were submitted to the Securities and Exchange Commission with my application to approve funding."

"How did the clearance of the prospectus go?" Fred asked Rick.

"It was an uphill battle. The SEC wasn't comfortable with how funding works. I'm not sure I'm comfortable with how Equity Funding does it, either. There were a lot of reinsurance documents in their file, but it's hard to tell from those documents how they did it. On the last day of the hearing, we got down to two questions. First, how are the loans going to be made? Second, why should we be exempted from their rule prohibiting the use of the history of mutual funds to demonstrate future performance?

Fred asked, "How did you get around those issues?"

"I answered their first question about the loans by referencing the reinsurance contracts and argued that the various state insurance commissioners have unique jurisdiction of both insurance and lending within a life insurance contract. Recognizing the previously approved funding by Equity Funding Corporation, the commission decided not to pursue that issue. But they dug their heels in on us using history as typical of mutual fund growth."

Jim slammed his hand on the table. "You've got to be kidding. What's their problem with our sales material?"

"It assumes mutual funds will grow an average of three percent each year on a long-term basis, just like they have in past decades, but it is well-established that one may not sell a security based on its past performance."

"You mean the SEC says we cannot assume a three percent annual growth for mutual funds, even though inflation is at twelve percent right now?"

"That's right."

Jim walked over to Jim's chair and held out his hand. "Great Job, Rick. Keep up the good work."

Fred ended the meeting. A big smile reached across his face. "Let's fold on that issue, and get back to recruiting. We've got funding coming!"

***

To implement his expansion plans, Fred needed to raise cash for the company. He hung his suit coat on the rack in the corner of his office, loosened his necktie, ran his fingers through his hair, and took a sip of the coffee waiting for him on his desk. He lit a Marlboro then asked his secretary to put in a phone call to Marco Flynn.

"Marco," Fred said as he blew out a puff of smoke, "How are things going in your part of the country these days? Are you still traveling a lot? And how's Susan?"

"Slow down, Fred. I've flown with you long enough to know when you have something on your mind besides my family and me. What's up?"

"I want to run an idea by you. My move to California as General Agent for Pioneer Life is not working out the way I hoped it would. I'm talking about financial planning. You and I discussed that before I took the job."

"Yeah, we did, Fred. I wondered how you were going to put life insurance and financial planning together without bruising some shoulders. I knew you'd need more capital. What's happening?"

"Frankly, my financial planning objective is looking less likely as time goes on. I've finally got funding on the table. You're right. I need to get some long-term financing to move ahead with funding. I slowed down my quest for a better way to serve clients across this country and promised myself I'd never let any of my clients get themselves into a mess like John DeFay. Not on my watch."

"Who the hell is John DeFay?"

"He owned that dry cleaner near my house. John died unexpectedly and left a wife and three children with no money. He neither had life insurance nor mutual funds. All he had was the store and some stocks. The stocks went to hell just before his death.

"I tried to get him to come into the office and make plans for his family, but he was always too busy. I failed him, Marco. He died with no financial protection for his family. I swore I'd never let that happen again.

"The financial services system still needs fixing—brought up to date, not thrown out. Funding is an important step in that direction, and Forrest Senf is developing insurance policies that contain funding. We got it cleared with the Securities and Exchange Commission and are now working to have those policies approved by state insurance departments. I don't think I can pursue my ultimate objective much longer without some serious working capital. Do you have any ideas?"

"I think you're on the right track," Marco said. "I've been thinking about your playing field. You're between a rock and a hard place. I want to come out there and help you, old buddy, but you know that I'm on a short string at home. Susan's father wanted me to join his law firm when I graduated from Stanford Law School. I upset him when I told him I planned to open own my law practice. Haven't talked to him much since."

"Sorry about that. It takes two."

"But my decision paid off. My law practice is doing well. Susan isn't happy with my travel schedule and has her suspicions about my entertainment choices on the road, but she keeps them to herself. I'll give some thought to your idea and how I can help you get some cash."

"I'll appreciate that, Marco. By the way, the anniversary with our old Marine Corps Flight Squadron at Cherry Point is this month. Are you going?"

"Sure am. Neither of us has missed an annual squadron get-together in quite a while. That is until you moved out to the West Coast last year.

"Peggy and I will be there."

"I'm going to take a break from financing and watch the birds fly while the squirrels hide their winter nuts. But I'll be there to hear all the old war stories."

"Marco, I'd like to have $250,000 available to set up a corporation while I wait for funding," Fred said. "What do you think the chances are of getting some guys to give a personal guarantee for a line of credit from Wells Fargo Bank?"

"I think one or two of them could be amenable. Let me pitch it for you. All the guys know you. Several flew with you when you were on active duty. They know how focused you get when you decide on something. I think that's what made you a great fighter pilot. Let me give it some thought."

Fred and Marco went to Cherry Point, North Carolina, for the annual Marine squadron reunion. The other pilots, a little older now, were still full of vim and vigor. The celebration went on for two memorable days. Many attendees brought their wives, talked about old times, and discussed their current projects.

Marco had delivered his notes and some financial information about Fred's project to four of the Marines who would be on the trip.

"I told them you are looking for help to get a line of credit so you can get a new company going. I said their guarantees would help you. Those guarantees would terminate when the Company got formalized, and some of the proceeds from its subsequent initial public offering (IPO) of stock could be used to repay the loan. Their guarantees would then be released."

As the group gathered on the first day at Cherry Point, Fred and Marco met with the four men who had responded to Marco about helping

Fred raise money. Marco had told each of them that he doesn't think Fred needs the money at this time. He wants to be prepared to have cash available if he needs it."

Peter Haskins stepped forward after Fred finished his presentation. "Count me in," he announced. "I think Fred's riding a winner. Can I buy some stock in your new company?"

"Not at this time," Fred answered. "But you can buy some stock at our initial private stock offering. That should be after I get the company set up."

With that, Jim Petersen stood up and said, "Well, if Pete's in, count me in too."

Marco stepped to the center of the group and announced, "Well then, with two more Fred could get a guarantee for $50,000 each, and I'll take the last $50,000. Our liability would be individual, not joint—each man would only be responsible for the amount of his guarantee."

Not to be left behind, Tom Johnson jumped in. "Hey, wait. I'm in too."

Before Marco or Fred could respond, Luke McCarter piped in. "Well, don't leave me out, guys. The way I count it with five of us in, we will each only be guaranteeing part of Fred's individual $250,000 credit line."

"Time out," Fred said. "Let's slow down. Marco, is that right? Would the guarantees be personal guarantees? There would several take-downs against the credit line by Fred, combined for the entire $250,000—-but not combined for the total amount of the line of credit by any one individual?"

"I think so," Marco replied. "But let me get back to you after I return to my office and check it out."

The annual reunion was a roaring success for the former Marine Squadron pilots.

Fred and Peggy headed home on an American Airways plane to wait for next year's squadron get-together. Fred promised to set next year's meeting at the Meadow Club in Marin County where they could get in a little golf on a signature course loaded with history.

"It always feels good to be a Marine," Fred told Peggy as they settled into their seats. "And I have some even better news for you, Peggy. Marco might put his law practice on hold to work with me for a while."

"You've got to be kidding." Peggy smiled as she fastened her seat belt. "I didn't think Marco would ever leave Florida. I'll never get used to the way you consistently pull things off."

"*Semper fi.*" Fred's said with a wink.

***

It had been an unusually hot summer. Traffic moved in and out of The City across the Golden Gate Bridge. Rick gazed out of his picture window at Hoskins and Woodford. The morning fog had retreated to the ocean, and an oil tanker, probably on its way to China, headed toward the Pacific. The notification on Rick's telephone bleeped for the second time. He picked it up.

"Hi, Rick. Fred Maloney here. Do you have time for lunch? I can't promise cuisine like we had at the Tadich Grill, but I have a twelve-thirty reservation at Scoma's on Fisherman's Wharf. Jim Barns is in town. Can you join us?"

Scoma's was near his office on the Embarcadero. Rick glanced at his Day-Timer. "Love to."

Rick took the elevator down and turned north on Jackson Street toward Fisherman's Wharf. The morning fog had drifted back to the ocean. Seagulls surveyed the piers and docks for scraps of food, and the sun shone between the puffy white clouds backdropped by the California blue sky.

Things have been going well these past few months. I'm back to practicing law. My office is beautiful. Rick navigated his way through the magnificent buildings down Bush Street, over toward Market Street.

Gloria loves her new surroundings in Marin County, and the daily trip to my office is only forty-five minutes. If I take the ferry, the drive is fifteen minutes from home. Life is good.

***

On the wooden deck atop the famous seafood restaurant, Fred and Jim stood at the rail overlooking the marina. The sound of waves in the harbor blended with the call of seagulls returning from their morning catch. The men chose a quiet table with a view of the marina and watched the fishing boats rock gently in the water below.

Fred, dressed in slacks and a crisp blue shirt, was in good shape. Rick and Jim—at six foot two—both towered over Fred, but Fred had that feature of leadership that overcame physical characteristics and allowed him to focus his listeners on his proposal.

Jim was the model of a strong, healthy man—muscular and coordinated. He wore his thick brown hair neat and combed back.

Rick was always dressed well, stood straight, and gave his full attention on the goal. Most women passing back and forth couldn't help but notice the three sharp-looking men.

Fred introduced Jim to Rick. As Fred surveyed his two companions, he recalled advice he had received earlier from the CEO of a major conglomerate. *When selecting an executive, if you must choose between intellect and persistence, favor persistence every time.* Fred noted the look of determination he saw in Jim's eyes. Jim was ready to listen, and Fred had confidence in Rick's persistence. *We would make quite a team,* Fred told himself.

Fred lit his cigarette and sat down. Jim and Rick pulled chairs to the table and joined him. As the well-endowed waitress approached, Jim commented, "Check her out. Too bad she won't be joining us for lunch on such a beautiful day."

The young waitress came to their table, a white napkin draped over her left arm. "We're offering some fine Napa Valley Chardonnay for our lunch menu."

"I'll take whatever you give me," Jim said with a wink.

Fred shot him a look. *Again with the pitiful come-on?*

Jim shrugged.

"Do you recommend it for the calamari?" Fred asked.

"A fine pairing."

"Sounds good. Please bring us a bottle of the chardonnay along with calamari."

Scoma's was not crowded. The light sea breeze created a peaceful atmosphere with the fishing boats swaying back and forth. While enjoying their lunch, Fred told Rick about the progress he and Jim had made in their individual recruiting.

"We both now know that funding is coming to Pioneer Life," Fred said. "Jim is ready to sign a Pioneer Life contract so he can sell those policies. He'll still keep his West Coast Life contract in effect, but he will be selling Pioneer Life insurance to those agents who want funding. We still don't know how long that will take. Jim is convinced commissions will continue to be the primary motivator for the mutual fund representatives as opposed to financial planning. But our focus will now be on recruiting with funding."

The waitress flipped back her flowing brown locks and poured Napa Valley Chardonnay into each wine glass. The pairing proved irresistible.

Lunch was delicious, and the surroundings added to the ambience.

While waiting for their dessert, Fred got down to business. "The financial services industry has had its way long enough."

"The salesmen will need more motivation than advisory fees can provide," Jim added. "The industry views investment advice as a contradiction in terms. Merrill Lynch Pierce Fenner and Smith push reps to emphasize the investments that Merrill Lynch sponsors—usually their securities. They may sell other products, but the incentives point to Merrill Lynch products. And banks will only loan money if you can pass their qualification tests."

Fred and Jim agreed that the loans provided by funding would be an attractive feature to new customers.

"We can build a company by introducing nontraditional financial products, like financial planning, no-load mutual funds, and even the introduction of advisory fees. Financial seminars will make that easier," Fred said.

Jim said, "We'll have our hands full adjusting to marketing life insurance with funding along with mutual funds.

"I want to combine our sales efforts into a single sales company and focus on funding," Fred replied.

As the desserts arrived, Jim took a long look at the waitress and accidentally knocked over his ice water. The men used napkins to soak up the water while the waitress went for towels.

"Jesus, Jim," Fred said. "You act like a teenage boy."

"What can I say. Women are beautiful, and I'm young at heart."

As the waitress dabbed the table with a towel, Fred got to the main point. "Rick, we need a corporate attorney. Jim and I have decided if we throw our businesses together, we can both grow faster with funding. Our CPA firm, David Walsh & Company, recommends that we incorporate. Jim will be licensed with both Pioneer Life and West Coast Life. We'll recruit together for the new Pioneer Life policies. We need a corporation that manages the funding for the life insurance and mutual fund sales the two of us produce."

Jim agreed. "We need legal help, which is very expensive in San Francisco."

"Jim and I already knew this would be a hard sell," Fred added. "So, we come to you with an offer you can't refuse." Fred looked at Rick. "We want you to be our general counsel—and a shareholder. You can do some of our work at home and still handle your regular legal business with Woodford and Hoskins at the office."

"An interesting thought." Rick pulled his chair back from the table, picked up his cup of coffee, and looked at both men. "What do you have in mind?"

"In addition to all of our business assets, Jim and I will each contribute $100,000 cash for our common stock in the new corporation. Rick, you take ten percent of the stock for your legal advice. Jim and I will split the rest. That way, neither Jim nor I will have a majority interest. You won't be an employee, but you can bill the company for costs."

"Boy, you sure don't let any grass grow under your feet." Rick stroked his chin. "Let me discuss this with Gloria."

They got up from their chairs and shook hands. Fred paid the tab while Jim and Rick small talked.

***

Rick Taylor headed back toward the Alcoa Building. On the horns of a dilemma, Rick knew Gloria wouldn't like the offer, yet he wanted to help Fred. *I'm sure that Gloria will object if I work more. The commute alone takes time each day. If I put the corporation together over a weekend, she'll have the extra pressure caring for three children while I work. When I tell her we'll get some free stock in the new company, I don't think she'll care.*

Yes, we have an agreement that I get to make the business decisions, but she will probably say this is where she puts her foot down. I can hear her now, "We have plenty of money from the time you already put in for work."

Damn it; I want to help Fred; this will be an exciting chance for us. Fred and I have already invested so much time working that Gloria and I didn't even take vacations. Maybe I could offer her a trip to Hawaii, either with or without the children, if she lets me take the job.

Friday evening. When Rick walked into the kitchen, Gloria had just finished making oatmeal cookies. She looked happy, following a day of cleaning house and caring for the children. He kissed her on the cheek, and without saying a word, took her apron and hung it up. He then reached for her hand and led her into the living room where they took seats on the couch.

Here goes, Rick thought. He told Gloria about the meeting with Fred Maloney and Jim Barns. Her mood changed.

"What about Woodford and Hoskins?" Gloria stood up, stomped across the room, and faced Rick. "You finally got the job you've wanted. How is this going to work out? And what's the point of ten percent of the stock in a corporation that doesn't even exist?"

Rick's mind whirled with ways to calm the situation. "That's what we need to decide, sweetheart."

"Don't sweetheart me," she snapped.

"Give me a sec here," Rick muttered. "Their proposal is interesting and speculative, but I think it might work out. The new corporation wouldn't employ me—I'd be 'of counsel' and still be employed full time by Woodford and Hoskins. I can do the new company's legal work at home. I'll have to run it by the law firm, of course, but I think taking it on as a part-time job would work. I'll call Jim Hoskins tomorrow." Rick reached into his shirt pocket for a cigarette.

"I'll get some coffee." Gloria tucked in her chin and headed for the kitchen.

When she returned to the couch, Rick noted the glare in her eyes. *Looks like I'm in trouble. I haven't seen that expression on her face in a long time. Maybe never. I think it will work out. I have to soften the blow.*

"Well, what are you going to do now?" she asked. "Be a part-time father? This will take even more time away from the family." Her eyes narrowed further. "I always told you I'd go along with whatever job you wanted, and I have. We've always decided together on what is best for the family. I haven't heard much this evening of what I call 'best for the family.' You have a good job with the law firm, but now you are sacrificing family time." Her tears flowed, and her voice was unsteady.

They talked it over all weekend long. Gloria canceled her previous plans for a family picnic on Saturday. She was frustrated and knew that the paint had already dried on the wall—Rick was hooked.

Finally, with some reluctance, she agreed. "You call Mr. Hoskins, Rick. I'll move our family picnic over to the following weekend."

***

On Wednesday, Fred, Jim, and Rick gathered at the Palace Hotel at 2 New Montgomery Street in San Francisco. That morning, Rick gave up his usual stop at the Bush Street peanut shop where he always bought cashews for his day at the office. Fred and

Jim were already waiting when he arrived at the Palace. Too early for lunch at the Garden Court, the men decided they would talk first, and then have lunch. Luxurious chairs and couches were available in the magnificent setting at that hotel.

Fred selected a comfortable chair adjacent to the long hallway at the front of the building. Rick took the other chair, and Jim sat on the crimson couch closer to the entrance. Within minutes, an attendant brought coffee. Fred lit his usual Marlboro. Rick took a cigarette from his shirt pocket, and joined him.

"No cigarette for me," Jim said when offered one. "I'm interested in maintaining my health." He then added several spoonfuls of sugar to his coffee.

Rick and Fred passed a covert smile.

"This will be the first meeting of the board of directors of our new corporation at the Palace Hotel in the City of San Francisco," Fred said. "Take it, Rick."

"As you may have surmised," Rick said, "Gloria's concern is my legal career."

"Does that mean it's a no?" Fred muttered.

Rick shrugged, opened his briefcase, and pulled out more papers. He handed out copies of his notes and asked them, "Have you picked a name yet?"

"Capital Funding Corporation," Jim responded. "Everyone knows we'll be competing with Equity Funding Corporation. The recruits I talk with will be excited we'll be offering funding. No other company does; we'll be the second. Equity's stock keeps going through the roof on the American Stock Exchange. That will help when we sell some of ours."

Fred jumped in. "Hold on, Jim. Don't forget about the tortoise and the hare. It'll be a long journey, and we have to be in shape for it. Funding is only a recruiting step; the mission is financial planning for the middle class. This is not a paratrooper military assault. We have many steps to take before we get to the top of this mountain."

"I need a name to file the papers," Rick said. "I don't know whether the name Capital Funding Corporation will pass muster with the California

Department of Corporations because of the similarity of names. We'll have to file to find out."

Jim paused. "I'd like to have a name listed at the beginning of the phone book. Let's get one that starts with an 'A.' One that's easy for potential recruits to remember.

Considering the steps Forrest had taught Fred, he said, "Our first step has got to be a name for the company. I think we ought to file for Capital Funding and see what happens. The alphabet's not as important as having a name that tells the public what we're about," Fred replied. "Trust is at the heart of financial relationships. We're not just selling products.

"We'll need to set tools and standards for financial planning. Planners will need a questionnaire to survey the client's data, list the client's goals, then analyze and evaluate that information. Then comes the discussions about alternatives with the client. Once these financial advisers implement the plan, they'll provide ongoing monitoring for the client."

"That's a long way from just selling life insurance and mutual funds," Jim added. "It'll take time and a lot of work before we get there. Clients need to learn how to plan. Magic Johnson found a way. Magic's financial advisors used the current high-interest rates and bet on inflation. The strategy worked magic. Pardon the pun. Their advice produced a five-year contract with the Los Angeles Lakers paying Johnson twenty-five million dollars a year to play basketball. That's the largest basketball salary ever."

"Our clients might not be basketball fans, Jim, but they still have to learn how to plan their estates."

Rick cut that conversation short. "How about American Financial Planning Corporation?"

"That's it!" Jim said. He glanced at Rick and smiled. It was apparent he was impressed. "We're on a roll now."

"Excellent," Fred added. "I forgot that lawyers are also salesmen."

"Okay, then, I'll apply for that name. These draft articles of incorporation," Rick said as he passed out documents, "authorizes two million shares of common stock. We should leave room for later sales, especially our own sales force. We'll issue 150,000 shares to Fred, 150,000 shares to Jim, and 20,000 shares to me. That makes 320,000 shares issued or 51% of the issued shares. No one individual will have control of the company.

"We also need to set up a subsidiary corporation that can handle the mutual fund sales and register it as a securities broker-dealer. The shares will be issued to American Financial Planning Corporation. Please take these papers with you, and let me know what questions you have."

"Do we need documents to transfer our equipment, our business licenses, and income to the corporation?" Jim asked.

"Yes. I'll prepare them. We'll open a corporate bank account to receive your deposits and to deposit corporate income. Jim suggested we use the initials for the broker-dealer subsidiary we'll need, and I agree. I'll file for approval of the name AFPC Securities Company. You two are paying cash for your shares. I will have stock issued to me in consideration of legal services rendered. Any more discussion or questions?"

Fred smiled. "I move we accept Rick's recommendations and close this meeting."

"Motion carried. The board meeting is adjourned."

***

Rick left the Palace Hotel, stepped onto Market Street, and reviewed this important day. *Just as America is no longer the only player in the post-World War II world, the financial services industry can no longer call all the shots. We are pioneers. For the first time since the 19th Century, America is becoming a debtor nation that faces sharp competitive pressure from a revitalized Germany and Japan. We must do what we can to get this country going again.*

Mark Twain said, "Years from now, you will be more disappointed by the things you didn't do than by the ones you did. So, throw off the bowlines, sail away from the safe harbor, and catch the trade winds in your sails. Explore. Dream. Discover." I have those words printed on the back of my business card.

I need to remember that there's no assurance Fred can achieve his dream. And I've got the family to take care of. What the hell am I doing? I know it's a stretch, but I have a gut feeling about these two guys—-a good gut feeling. I can handle the home situation with Peggy and will spend more time with the kids.

CHAPTER SIX
Foot Soldiers

Jim Barns drove to the Inland Empire to start looking for agents. Fred spent the next few weeks talking to agents and registered representatives between Sacramento and Los Angeles. When he returned to San Francisco, Fred called Jim and Rick Taylor for a meeting, and invited the company's Chief Financial Officer, Bud Johnson, to join them in the conference room.

When Fred walked in, he crushed his Marlboro into the ashtray, looked at his assembled team, and said "It's time to let our sales force enjoy part of what we are accomplishing. Rick, what do we have to do to get them some of our stock?"

The conference room was silent as they selected chairs around the table. With its new furniture, the conference room looked like a real boardroom. Mahogany bookshelves, filled with reference manuals and books, surrounded the long table and leather chairs. The secretary had placed fresh flowers from a street vendor onto the shinning table. Through the large glass windows, one could see shoppers milling up and down on Market Street, which stretched out below them. A streetcar picked up shoppers.

Rick took the seat next to Fred and opened his briefcase. The mimeograph machine hummed in the background. A new employee made photocopies of the agenda for everyone and placed them next to each yellow pad.

Fred called the meeting to order. "There's only one item on the agenda today, gentlemen. We need to give our sales force something to look forward to besides hard work. They need an opportunity to buy some of our common stock and have more of an interest in who we are and where we are going."

"New life and mutual fund sales are going well," Bud Johnson told the group. "Financially, the company can justify a common stock offering. Our income statement looks pretty good."

Rick took over. "With nonpublic or private stock, we don't have to go through the full registration process with the Securities and Exchange Commission. However, we still have to get approval from the California Department of Corporations. The reason we can sell private stock to specific buyers without registration is that SEC Rule 506 allows a sale of common stock to up to 35 individuals who don't otherwise qualify as accredited investors.

"What's an accredited investor?" Jim asked.

Rick continued. "The SEC adopted Regulation D for accredited investors. That regulation allows an investor who is deemed sophisticated enough about financial matters, and sufficiently wealthy, to investigate the private stock he wants for himself. National securities exchange does not list private stock. Regulation D gives companies a limited window to raise capital from small sales of their stock without going through the full federal and state registration and qualification process.

"For our purposes, there is a further exemption for up to 35 individuals who are not 'sophisticated investors' but want to buy our stock. We'd list stocks on the over-the-counter market—its name on the street, or the 'pink sheets.'

"The California Department of Corporations must okay the stock sale, but I can handle that locally. To answer your question, Jim, yes. We can sell our stock—within the thirty-five-person limit. However, right now, we don't see eye to eye with the California Department of Corporations on the offering price."

Excited, Fred didn't even pick his smoking cigarette up from his ashtray. "I think we could raise maybe $350,000 in a private placement with just the salespeople we already have and a few friends. Some of our sales managers would like to buy a block of stock, including my old Marine Corps buddy, Marco Flynn, back in Florida. Nobody has to buy stock, but I don't want to leave any of our salespeople out in the cold if they want to purchase some."

Jim agreed. "You're right, Fred. A few of our managers could come up with the money, but I agree that we should spread it out. Private placement with 35 buyers at $10,000 apiece would raise $350,000 for the company. Let's talk about it with the managers."

When put to them by Fred and Jim, an enthusiastic response came from branch managers. They had been following Equity Funding's stock price movement as a positive indication for funding. Fred and Jim both believed that the demand for American Financial stock would be substantial. Fred was concerned that the company would have more requests for stock than he had planned to sell.

The stock was listed in the over-the-counter market on the pink sheets. It started out at five dollars a share, but by the end of the first month, the price of the stock had passed eight. Although stock held by the three directors of the company could not be sold for some time, there were no restrictions on a stockholder re-selling his stock to someone else.

The price on the pink sheets varied when stock was bought or sold. The stock price continued to climb. By the end of the third month, it passed thirty-six dollars a share. Fred savored the reactions from his branch managers following the stock sale.

***

A motivated sales force took the bit in its teeth and roared forward. Life insurance production sprouted. Mutual fund sales were close behind. As the Company's private stock price in the pink sheets grew, Fred considered an offering of company stock to raise public funds, but an initial public offering (IPO) would take time to qualify and register. Besides, the company would need more assets, and an audit, before an initial public offering could be put together.

Fred and Jim pulled up chairs in Fred's Pioneer Life office conference room. They spread their recruiting notes and Rolodex filing systems on the table.

"Funding is now the primary catalyst for recruiting new insurance agents, and the price of the stock in the pink sheets is a great retainer."

Although Fred agreed, he saw things differently. He hoped funding would blossom and create more of an interest in financial planning. Fred turned his Rolodex back to its beginning and suggested that they start with the letter "A."

"Nope. There are no names under A in my file," Jim said. "I've gotta meeting coming up with John Brown in San Jose. You know John—he's got a strong team in both life insurance and mutual fund sales in the South Bay. They sell a hell of a lot of Boston mutual funds. He'd be a great financial planner. We might get him to work with us, but he is not motivated to make a change. Midwest Securities Company pays for his comfortable office. I'll see how he'd go for this advisor fee business you want to introduce."

Fred said, "Show him how he can be his own boss again by working with us. We should build a new sales force focused on both life insurance and mutual funds, now that we have funding. We need to generate some new income for American Financial."

A look of relief swept across Jim's face. Fred knew Jim still believed reps preferred those commissions.

"Financial planning may be the wave of the future, but reps live in the present," Jim said. He admitted seminars did a great job attracting potential customers for the mutual fund reps. "Having lawyers talk about financial planning at the seminars is a great attraction as well.

"John and I go back a long way. He's a good man," Jim continued. "We've kept in touch. I'd love to see him become our San Jose branch manager. He's got a nice office and a secretary he doesn't have to pay for; we can't afford to do that.

I've known John since we double-dated at a mixer at Santa Clara University. John's girl, a real beauty, snuggled up with me when we switched partners during the dance, but John married the date I had that night."

***

Jim met John Brown at the Orange Grove shopping center in San Jose. They ordered glazed doughnuts and coffee, then pulled chairs up to the patio table.

The bright morning sun lit the sky as commuters searched for pastries to take on the train. Jim told John about the new corporation he'd put together with Fred.

"American Financial now offers funding through Pioneer Life," Jim said.

John's eyes sparkled, and his generous smile featured his strong white teeth. "I can't believe it. I wanted funding, but couldn't motivate myself to move to Equity Funding." John Brown and Jim Barns—considered top producers for Boston Funds—both sold insurance for several life insurance companies.

They gave their view of the terrible economy and expressed their frustration. When would it end? Jim went through the other products that his new company offered.

"Still putting all that sugar in your coffee," John said. "Reminds me of the good old days in college."

Jim sat comfortably, his shoulders straight, his smile contagious. "What can I say? I liked my coffee on the sweet side." Jim winked.

"I'm happy with the product line I already have, Jim, but policies with funding; you've got my attention," John said. "I'm damn comfortable with my nice office, secretary, and investment products everyone's familiar with."

"Your customers *should* be familiar with them, John; they check *The Wall Street Journal* to see how their investments are doing." Jim emptied his paper coffee cup and dropped it into the trash can. "Fred Maloney and I are riding the crest of a wave with our introduction of asset management fees as part of the agent's income."

"Okay," John said. "I have eleven salesmen—some of them are unhappy, but it's mostly the economy that has them down. I'm not sure they'd like this fee-for-service approach. They're used to high commissions." He paused as though thinking. "Come on by the house tonight, Jim; we can throw steaks on the grill and talk."

"I'll be there with a bottle of Cabernet to go with those steaks," Jim replied. "We can also figure out when this bear market will end."

It was an enjoyable evening. Jim got to meet John's lovely family and played a game of checkers with John's son. After dinner was cleared, they spread documents across the table and discussed American Financial. John assured Jim he'd give the move serious thought.

***

In San Francisco, Phil Schmidt prepared to get off the cable car at the next street corner. It was at the end of the line. Up next, California Street, as the cable car headed back to Van Ness Avenue at the top of the hill.

Phil, a stockbroker with Merrill Lynch, also offered retirement plans that included life insurance, stocks, and bonds. Rather than waiting for a diversified portfolio of stocks in a mutual fund to fulfill its promise, Phil preferred active stock and bond trading. He leaned against the corner of an office building and perused the morning *Wall Street Journal* while he waited for Fred. "Will this slaughter ever stop?" Phil said to no one.

"Sorry Phil, but I don't have a calendar for the market. You'll have to hang in there." Fred said as he approached Phil. He shook Phil's hand then put his hand on Phil's shoulder. "Good to see you, buddy."

Phil folded his *Journal*, put it under his arm, and walked with Fred to the Commonwealth Club.

"They don't have a ticker tape in the members' guest room," Fred said with a wink.

"Sounds good to me," Phil replied.

At the Club, they found two overstuffed leather chairs near a window at the far end of the carpeted room. Hot coffee, orange juice, and pastries sat on a long table near the door. Through the large window was a great view of auto and cable car traffic carrying workers to their daily jobs.

"I enjoyed the talk you gave at the life underwriters' meeting last week," Phil said. "It made me consider focusing more on life insurance—especially with funding now available—while this stock market keeps its roller coaster ride. Your demonstration of seminars and overheads impressed me."

They lit cigarettes.

Fred inhaled, exhaled, and blew out a stream of smoke. "As a securities rep, you focused on individual life insurance and retirement plans for small business owners—like I did when I lived in Florida. Jim Barns and I are starting a new company that includes funding. American Financial will allow you to build up that portion of your business and move toward financial planning for your clients."

"I don't need anything new. I need something old—a reliable stock market. I don't think Merrill Lynch will offer the new no-load mutual funds becoming available."

"Merrill Lynch," Fred pointed out, "wants you to buy and sell stocks then charge the customer a commission going in and coming out. But the customer can limit the erratic market if he invests in mutual funds." Fred took a sip of the hot coffee, blew on it several times, and took a gulp. "That's what your customers should be doing anyway, Phil. With a no-load fund, the customer only pays a charge if he gets out early. That's also why customers buy life insurance—to protect their family. The two solutions are tied together. Without commissions to pay every time he buys or sells a stock, no-load funds will grow faster, and keep the customer's costs low.

"One day, the American Financial salesforce won't just be those who sell life insurance or mutual funds. There will be full-fledged financial planners. We'll learn how to plan in this horrid economy. They'll work *with* their client to define long-range objectives—not just tell him what to buy or sell. The advisor will create a plan to implement the customer's goals using simple investments—like inexpensive mutual funds—while protecting their families with affordable life insurance.

"Most of mid-America doesn't understand mutual funds, and they're scared to death of the stock market these days. The first job? Explain that a mutual fund is a bundling of the common stocks of many corporations. Your salesmen will show how owning small shares of stock in a mutual fund allows the client to be an owner of many corporations rather than trying to pick the stock of only one or two. The only way the investment markets will work is to have a long-time investing horizon; they can't get rich trying to play the market's ups and downs."

They emptied their coffee cups and were about to leave the club when Fred shook Phil's hand. "Jim Barns believes you have the foresight to be your own boss. We want you to come in with us. We need a San Francisco Branch Manager. You can build your *own* business, rather than Merrill Lynch's business. I think we could be a good fit for your positive lifestyle."

"Hmm, the idea is interesting and intriguing. Let me think about it."

Fred felt sure he'd hit a nerve. He had a strong sense Phil would become the San Francisco branch manager.

***

Jim continued traveling south across the state. He recruited Ron Farrow in San Bernardino. Ron knew Equity Funding well and had watched its stock grow.

"Now that American Financial has funding," he told Jim, "I'd be willing to make a new start.

There's no problem moving my license, but I won't agree to be a branch manager until I test funding with a few prospective clients.

***

Fred had used some draw-downs from his line of credit at the Wells Fargo Bank to provide more cash to the company. The additional $350,000 raised in the private offering provided enough capital to implement and expand the aggressive recruiting plans. However, the national economy continued to worsen. Risk capital was scarce. The newspapers and periodicals regularly reported fear of another Great Depression.

Life insurance sales went well, but new investments in mutual fund shares declined each week. Several companies made inroads into financial services with no-load mutual funds. T. Rowe Price offered a Balanced Fund, and Vanguard produced their Explorer Fund. Investment advisers continued to search such offerings and look for a new way to bring no-load funds to market.

Fred took these trends as additional confirmation that his ultimate goal of financial planning by and for the properly educated consumer was not lost. It was time to get to work on the basics with American Financial Planning Company—selling life insurance and mutual funds through educational seminars. Even with the company's stock performing well, they needed more cash to expand the growth of the sales force in additional states. Many of the recruits were independent businessmen who worked out of their homes with a part-time secretary. Branch managers needed office help. Money for seminars and traveling was a must.

***

Fred decided to call Marco Flynn, whose strength in corporate finance made him a good choice. *What we need is long-term capital so we can tee it up and slam it. I was a little concerned when Marco told me he kept an eye on our stock in the pink sheets. But he told me he'd buy some of our private stock when it came out. I asked him to be careful because we don't need and questions from either the State or the SEC about anyone playing around with our stock. He assured me he knows the law, and he will abide by it whenever he buys or sells our stock. Why did he say 'or sell' unless he is thinking about playing in that market? He knew Marco already owned a large amount of company stock.*

After checking with Marco on how things were at home, Fred told him that the company needed to borrow money. "I'd like to see if we can sell a bond to a sophisticated investor. I used the money from the line of credit you helped me obtain at Cherry Point. Thanks again for that.

"By the way, Marco, Pat Raab, one of my advisory committee members, has now moved from Mobile to San Francisco with the Wells Fargo Bank," Fred offered. "When I want advice, it will be easier for me to consult with him since he's in the local area now. Jim and I want to expand into surrounding states and boost our balance sheet with long-term capital. I know you've been involved in mergers and acquisitions in the Midwest from your law firm in Florida. Do you have any ideas?"

"Yeah, sure. The way you keep developing new plans, I knew you'd need more money. I've been thinking about Midwest Financial Corporation in Cincinnati. Charles De Long has grown that company and its financing operations. He's kept an eye on American Financial as a new start-up. To balance out his two Midwestern banks, he's acquiring various savings and loan associations. I know he likes Equity Funding—he made money in that stock. Mr. De Long might be a prospect for some long-term financing. How much do you want?"

"I'd like to get another $250,000 into the company—if it comes from the right source. I don't want somebody looking for a quick profit. Hell, I don't know Midwest Financial."

"Midwest Financial is a large conglomerate based in Cincinnati," Marco replied. "De Long wants to catch up with the other conglomerates and is always looking for deals. He owns banks and real estate, and he's well known for his philanthropy in the Cincinnati area. You can probably get a meeting if you call him. Do you have time to go to Ohio?"

Boy, that's a long way to go for a possibility. I would rather use the time recruiting. But I'm sure Marco didn't pull this idea out of his hat. "If you think it would be worthwhile, sure."

"I was involved in a deal that brought Mr. De Long a Florida bank. I think it's worth a shot. Give him a call."

"What'll I tell him?"

"Tell him who you are and what you want. He knows about your new company and has been watching your stock in the pink sheets. Say you need some additional capital for expansion in the Midwest and want to issue a $200,000 bond for the expansion program. Charles De Long likes to talk to the top man. Call him. Get acquainted on the phone. Tell him about your plans in Ohio—if you have any."

***

Fred and Charles De Long talked on the phone for almost an hour. Jim sipped on a cup of sugared coffee and ate two glazed doughnuts while he listened to the phone conversation.

Fred told Mr. De Long that American Financial planned to use the $200,000 to expand into the Midwest.

Charles De Long countered, "It's interesting. Come to Cincy, and we can talk about

it. I'll have a room available for you at the Best
Western Motel. Let my secretary know what time
you will arrive."

Fred hung up the phone.

Jim stood with fists clenched and face red.
"Fred, don't take the bait. Why the hell should you
take a long trip to Ohio without some
documentation or at least an expression of interest?
We're very busy with the sales force right now, and
I need your help."

"You're right. I don't want to run up a blind
alley. I wish Marco had offered to call Charles De
Long first to see what interest he might have. But he
thought I should call him directly. I have a lot of
confidence in Marco. He knows the financing
business. And he knows how Charles De Long
operates. All we have to lose is a weekend; I can
leave on Friday. Marco has an inkling that this
connection might bear fruit."

*Jim's upset—he thinks I'm leaving him at
the plate, and we'll lose time with him doing all the
recruiting while I'm gone. He has a point there. But*

a corporate bond would be good—saving our cash and not selling more stock.

"I don't give a damn about your Marco Flynn. You're not flying jets together anymore. Get real! Keep your eye on the prize. We need recruits; money will come later. I'm outta here." He stormed out and slammed the door behind him.

***

The next day, Fred flew to Cincinnati to meet Charles De Long. Cincinnati's winter was crisp and clear. Icicles hung from roofs, and bare trees reached toward the gray sky. Wooden logs, captured by frozen water, were in the motel swimming pool. Fred knew right away he favored California's dryer heat and sunshine.

An attorney and two secretaries set themselves up in the motel conference room on Saturday morning. Fred spoke with De Long by phone on Saturday and Sunday, but where was he? A coiled frustration settled in Fred's chest. The attorneys met with Fred and said Mr. De Long was away but planned to return to talk with Fred on Monday.

Rage shot through Fred. *Screw this. I'm heading to the airport. Jim was right. I'll call him and eat crow.* Fred packed his travel bag, then called Jim.

"Looks like you were right, Jim. I shouldn't have wasted my time."

Jim let Fred rant and rave for a few minutes and then, in a calm and collected voice said, "I was afraid of that. But, since you're already there, why don't you wait until Monday and hear what De Long has to say."

"Okay, Jim. I'll hang in through Monday. But if I don't have a plan I know we can live with, I'm on my way back."

The two secretaries stayed busy typing and passing paper drafts from the attorneys to Fred for his perusal. He made notes for his meeting with De Long. The amount was right: a $200,000 corporate bond. But, without Mr. De Long there, he couldn't discuss his concerns.

Fred didn't like the proposed plan—for Midwest Financial to buy a $200,000 ten-year, thirteen percent bond. That part was right, but the interest was too high. The documents also required that Fred and Jim pledge their stock in American Financial as additional security for the bond. That stopped Fred cold.

Already pissed about the thirteen percent interest on the bond, Fred called Jim and told him about the stock pledge requirement he'd just found—pledged to Charles De Long *as an individual*.

"I screwed up, Jim. I'm not even going to wait for Monday."

"I'm with you. To hell with Monday. Let De Long talk to himself. Come on home. You can still have time with Peggy on Monday evening."

Fred hung up. As if it were a basketball, he tossed his favorite pen and watched it miss the trash basket by a couple of feet. He grabbed the pen for one last try—but it hit the rim and fell to the carpet.

Trying to put a positive spin on the De Long debacle, Fred looked at the situation as a lesson learned. He chalked it up to experience, put it in his memory bank, and flew back to San Francisco. Fred later discovered Mr. De Long had been talking to him from his boat in the Cayman Islands.

CHAPTER SEVEN
Legal Issues

In mid-January, Fred opened a letter from a New York law firm stating that American Financial and its broker-dealer AFPC Securities Company's name was owned by its client, AFPC Industries, Inc. The document demanded that American Financial Planning Company stop the use of the name or logo AFPC.

Fred couldn't believe it! *We make one step forward and then back two. I should have just kept selling life insurance in Florida and Alabama.* Fred shook his head. *Who the hell are these guys? I've never heard of AFPC Industries. Sounds like an industrial company. This looks like an expensive law firm, so the company must be real. Where the hell are they coming from? I better take another look if we are going to start dealing with legal questions.*

Fred called Rick and read the letter he received.

"Hold on, Fred. Let me check this out." The phone went silent. "AFPC Industries, Inc. is one of the many subsidiaries of Gulf +Western Incorporated, a large New York conglomerate. AFPC is a subsidiary of theirs, dealing in raw materials—they make and sell cement."

Fred was angry. "Rick, their letter demands a response that lays out the steps we need to take to cease using the acronym AFPC for our broker-dealer. Within 30 days. Failure to do so requires their client to file a lawsuit in the Southern District of New York. Is this something you can help us with? Should we retain Woodford and Hopkins?"

Rick said, "I'll come over and evaluate the document. Make a photocopy for me."

Beside himself, Fred slammed his fist onto his desk. The vibration caused his ashtray to fall to the floor. Cigarette butts tumbled and ashes blended with the dark carpet. Fred squatted and placed the scattered butts into the ashtray. *Maintenance can get the ashes.* He slid the ashtray across the desk and sat.

Shocked that his new company might be sued, Fred called Jim in Pasadena. *Like I have time to screw around with a goddamn lawsuit.*

"We're not even in the same consumer markets," Jim said, his anger strung through his words like spiderwebs. "How could someone in their right mind confuse those two products?"

"Exactly."

"Now what?"

"Rick's on his way here right now," Fred replied. "I'll let you know."

As he traveled around the Inland Empire, Jim repeatedly called Fred to vent. None of the agents he knew had ever heard of AFPC Industries, Inc.

***

Rick researched the law and walked over to the American Savings building. "Don't worry," Rick offered. "We can continue to use our name. Our AFPC Securities Company is on record to do business in California, and they haven't even filed. We'll prevail if there is a lawsuit."

But their hopes were short-lived. AFPC Industries, Inc. would not let go. Letters back and forth between Rick and the New York law firm made no progress. Plus, another issue plagued Fred. American Financial couldn't afford the plane fare and hotel expenses needed to send Rick to New York to negotiate the lawsuit. Much of the company's money had already been spent sending Rick to Washington to clear the funding prospectus and for legal fees to Hoskins & Woodford.

The corporate records in Sacramento showed American Financial had the legal right to use the name AFPC Securities Company for its broker-dealer subsidiary. Neither the conglomerate Gulf+Western nor its subsidiary had bothered to register AFPC Industries, Inc. in California, even though they were doing business at their cement facility on the San Joaquin River in Stockton.

Fred called Keith Raab in New York.

"Keith, hope I have found you well and in good spirits," Fred said.

"I've been in good spirits ever since I retired from the Strategic Air Command." He laughed. "How are things going with your company? Did Jim get Phil Schmidt to make a move to American Financial?"

"We've been doing fine. And yes, Phil did come with us. He heads our San Francisco Branch. But just as we got our new marketing program together, I received a legal demand letter on behalf of a subsidiary of Gulf+Western Company named AFPC Industries, Inc. The letter demands we stop using *their* name for our broker-dealer subsidiary, AFPC Securities Company."

"*What*? I know Gulf+Western well. They have many subsidiaries in a variety of industries. But that name is a new one. What're you doing about it?"

"Rick Taylor believes the law is with us. There is no similarity between products or business between their company and our broker-dealer. Similar names would not confuse the public. And their name isn't even registered in California. Rick thinks we shouldn't have to change our name. But they will not relent."

"I'll talk to my friend Bob Jones to see if a compromise is possible. He's on Gulf+Western's board. And, he and I are both on the board of another New York company," Keith told Fred. "I'll give Bob a call."

"I appreciate anything you can do to help," Fred said. "We're convinced they're on the wrong track, but it's too costly for Rick spend time or money to go back to New York. And I don't want to hire a New York attorney at this juncture."

"Let me see what I can do."

***

Rick Taylor drafted a legal complaint to file against AFPC Industries in the San Francisco Federal District Court. His lawsuit charged Gulf+Western with illegally using the AFPC Securities Company's name in California and demanded they immediately cease from doing so. It also required money damages be awarded to American Financial by AFPC Industries. Rick got into his car, drove across the Golden Gate Bridge, and filed the lawsuit.

Thinking Keith Raab could use the certified copy of the complaint as a negotiating tool, he chose not to serve a copy on the defendant company.

***

Keith set up an informal meeting with his friend, Bob Jones. When Keith and Bob reviewed the background and the facts, they both agreed that it was "much ado about nothing." They didn't think there could be any confusion with both companies using the same logo or name. Gulf+Western agreed that its subsidiary made a mistake not filing the name in a state where they were doing business.

They reached a compromise.

Keith phoned Fred. "Here's the proposal, Fred. If you drop your lawsuit, they will not pursue theirs. As I told you, Bob Jones saw the merits of your position. He convinced an associate on the Gulf+Western board that their subsidiary is in error."

"Great job, Keith! Anything else involved in the settlement?"

"Yes. American Financial Planning Company must stop its use of AFPC, and rename its subsidiary Golden Gate Securities Company, the name you had suggested. To offset the cost of reprinting all the required marketing materials and stationery, AFPC Industries, Inc. will reimburse American Financial Planning Company for its costs—up to a maximum of $82,000."

"Wow, Keith! You should be on our board on a full-time basis," Fred said.

"Thanks, but no thanks. I would rather watch your progress from the sidelines."

***

Fred was not ready to give up on long-term capital—he wanted to sell either a bond or more common stock to strengthen the company's balance sheet. He asked Jim, Rick, and Marco—who was in town—to join him in the conference room. "I talked with Bill Breton in New York yesterday," he told them. "You remember Ralph Major at United American Life Insurance Company? He's the guy who introduced me to Bill Bretton."

Fred glanced around the room. Sunlight filtered in the window to form a halo of light. "Bill Breton is the Senior Vice President for mergers and acquisitions at United Express. He's curious about our growing sales force, but not enough to pursue anything at that time. He also expressed an interest in monitoring the company's common stock."

Jim threw his notebook onto the conference table; a grimace crossed his face. "Why the hell is a credit card company thinking about financial planning?" The muscles in his jaws clenched. One eyebrow raised.

Fred lit a Marlboro. "Calm down, Jim. The president, Howard Roberts, is thinking about the future. He wants to expand his customer base in the current uncertain economic environment. I think he may even consider a financial planning approach with seminars, to create a new customer base for his credit cards. He wants to build more cardholders in the Midwest."

"That's the dumbest thing I've ever heard," Jim snarled.

"Hold on," Fred tapped the cigarette tip, and a bit of ash landed in the ashtray. "When Bill Bretton and I met in San Francisco, I explained we would need more capital for our training efforts, especially for seminars. I think that opened a window for us to sell United Express on some long-term financing."

"C'mon, Fred. We already blew that one in Cincinnati. United Express has to sort out how their subsidiaries work on their own. While I agree we would love to sell them some of our stock, or even a bond, getting long-term financing from United Express is a long shot."

But I know Howard Roberts likes financial seminars. If I could meet him, I might see if he has an appetite for financial planning down the road. "I'm going to New York, Jim."

"What! What the hell for? We don't have anything going in New York. We have enough work west of the Rockies.

"I'm going to visit with Bill Bretton. They have a lot of interest in American Financial. I think they could be interested in buying some of our stock."

"You're out of your mind. We know what we can do out here. Is this advice from Marco Flynn again? Reminds me of Pearl Harbor. You've got to stop chasing rainbows."

***

When Fred got to the World Trade Center, he took the elevator to the top and greeted Bill Breton with a firm handshake.

"Nice to see you again, Fred. It's been a while."

"Great to see you too, Bill. What's the latest?"

"Howard Roberts feels you are on your way now. With that lawsuit behind you and your company to run, you have clear skies and good sailing ahead. He wants to get your thoughts on seminars."

"I'm looking forward to a conversation with him. By the way, we added attorneys to our seminars. It's been a real hit, and I think Howard will be interested in hearing about it. Customers love to hear the lawyers talk about estate planning without having to pay them for the advice. It's a win-win situation, and the lawyers often find new clients at our seminars."

"I'm pleased to hear such enthusiasm," Bill said. "I told Howard your ideas on incorporating seminars into the financial planning process. He's interested in offering some form of financial planning to get new credit card customers."

This works out even better than I hoped, Fred thought. *There's certainly room for credit cards in our seminars. And we need cash.*

The two men spent time discussing a new joint marketing plan that Bill had prepared for his life insurance and mutual fund subsidiaries. After reviewing the seminars Fred had created, Bill created a summary business plan and sent it to Howard Roberts.

Bill told Fred, "If United Express and American Financial sponsored joint seminars, we could offer products from both companies. Based on my recommendation to Howard and subject to approval by the executive committee, Howard has approved buying $300,000 of American Financial stock private stock as an investment."

This caught Fred off guard. *An investment? That's a long way from where Charles De Long was headed with his personal guarantees for our bond. Looks like we've finally got a shot at some solid long-term capital. I think Howard sees the possibility of other ways we can serve the public. Investment means stock—a private sale of private stock. Rick told me a transaction between two corporations could be accomplished without registration by the Securities and Exchange Commission.*

However, Henderson and Levy, two men on United Express' executive committee, worried about investing in a company that duplicated many of the products that United Express offered. Both corporations have competing subsidiaries in life insurance and mutual funds, which could be a problem. The committee understood that the mergers and acquisitions department had recommended an investment in American Financial Planning Corporation, and that Howard Roberts had agreed, subject to review by the committee. The other three members wanted to support the hard work Bill had put into this recommendation.

The debate caused the executive committee to extend its scheduled meeting time by another fifteen minutes. They knew Mr. Roberts was in South America and that he had recommended the investment to the committee before he left town. They had no way to get further insights into his thinking.

Mr. Roberts planned to return from his trip the day after the executive committee meeting had adjourned. The discussion had been long and heated. Ultimately, Henderson and Levy conceded, and the committee approved the purchase of American Financial stock.

Mr. Roberts returned the next day and called a few of his senior officers together—including Ken Rudd, the manager of the Boston mutual funds. After introducing Fred, he explained the essence of Fred's proposed marketing plan for financial seminars. "We'll work closely with American Financial Planning Corporation. Currently, they use seminars for marketing their life insurance and mutual funds." He turned to Ken Rudd and asked,

"How do you like the new sales force you'll be working with?"

With a frown on his face, Ken Rudd answered in a discouraged voice. "Nobody bothered to ask me, Mr. Roberts. I run the Boston mutual funds, not some guy from California who thinks he knows more about how to sell mutual funds than I do. I can handle the Boston mutual funds."

It was obvious he was upset. Perhaps he felt an unwanted intrusion into his assigned duties running his own subsidiary.

Mr. Roberts called for an immediate huddle. He didn't realize Ken had been left out of the discussions. Following a short conversation, he reported the executive committee's decision to buy American Financial common stock stood.

Fred shook hands with everyone, including Ken Rudd, and headed home a happy man. The United Express Company continued to hold American Financial stock for the next several years.

***

Back in California, Marco Flynn rented a room in Tiburon so he could work more conveniently with

American Financial Planning Corporation. The company's stock—now at $57 per share—had climbed rapidly. And with space available for him to work at the office, Marco felt he could contribute more if he spent additional time on the West Coast. He missed being with his family, but he could see that Fred would need more of his help. He wanted to be closer to the action.

But Marco had mixed emotions. He had no desire to break up his family. When he explained his plans to Susan, she broke out in tears.

"What's going on, Marco? Some of our friends say you're flirting with stewardesses. Is that true? What about the children and me?"

"I know a lot of talk goes around every time I get on a plane for business, Sue. But it's just talk. Sure, I enjoy looking at attractive girls—and lots of them fly around in airplanes. But it doesn't go any further than that. I love you, and I'll still be home often to see the kids. Fred needs my help with the company, and this temporary move will allow me to give him more time. You and the family will be safe while I am away. Never forget that you come first."

Marco knew Susan loved their home, the children were doing well in school, and everything was on track in Pensacola. And John Danford promised to keep an eye on the family when Marco was away.

"I'm sad that you won't be home as much, and I'm not happy with you renting an apartment. But I think I understand. You'll be home often?"

"Of course, I will, honey," Marco replied with a smile.

"You'll call every day?"

Marco took Susan in his arms. "Sure, I will. I love you."

Susan wiped the tears from her eyes. "I love you too."

The company planned its initial public offering (IPO) of common stock. Marco had been an active buyer of American Financial nonpublic stock since it was first issued. He knew Fred worried that he "played the market," but when asked about it, Marco told Fred he knew the rules on the pink sheets and was following them.

"I've always kept my eye on the daily pink sheets in search of good-sized amounts of stock offered by American Financial salesmen. Sellers of the stock were happy with the profits their stock enjoyed and wanted to cash some in and take the profits; I stood by as a willing buyer."

Since first offered to the American Financial field force, Marco had accumulated a large amount of American Financial private stock.

***

Insurance and fund production blossomed. Fred knew it was time for the company's initial public offering. Rick Taylor and Bud Johnson were at David Walsh & Company, the company's CPA firm. As Rick paged through American Financial's numbers with Ron Lindstrom, the CPA assigned to the company, Rick told him, "We don't agree with the California Securities Commissioner on the offering price for our IPO. You support us at $49 a share, but the Commissioner is stuck on $45. The pink sheets support the higher price, but all I hear from the California Department is our private shareholders are mostly officers or employees, not a public market, and that the California Corporations Commissioner doesn't give the pink sheet prices much weight."

"Back to the drawing board," Fred said as he sat down with Jim Barns and Rick Taylor. "Let's take another swing at the Department of Corporations. We're a company selling life insurance and mutual funds through our licensed subsidiary, Golden Gate Securities Company. We should emphasize our good relationships with several of the preeminent insurance and investments companies in the United States."

"I don't know if name dropping will help," Jim said, "But we have excellent personal relationships with several big names in both industries."

"Okay," Rick said. "But don't get your hopes up. I'll be sure to focuses on the quality of our securities subsidiary and its managers as well as our track record in the pink sheets. Let's set up a meeting with the California Corporations Commissioner and prepare to fight for the right price for our public stock offering."

***

"Jones and Petersen, the company's underwriter, supports the $49 initial offering price," Rick told the corporations examiner in the San Francisco office, who reminded Rick the corporation was new and, notwithstanding its private offerings, there's not enough capital in the corporation. "That's why we have a public offering," Rick replied.

Rick called Fred for advice.

"Could we appeal the decision?" Fred asked.

"We could, but that's another delay, and you'd probably have to review the financials again with David Walsh & Company.

They asked for one more meeting with the examiner after the weekend. The commissioner agreed to delay his ruling. On Monday, the commissioner told Rick the department's decision was final—there would be no negotiations.

Fifteen thousand shares of the stock went out at $47.50 per share for a $712,500 offering.

Fred and Jim were in Fred's office when Rick called. "We are now a public company, gentlemen. Hard work by our underwriters over the weekend paid off. Forty-seven dollars and fifty cents per share. We have raised $712,500."

By the end of the month, the stock closed at $51.45 per share on the Pacific Coast Stock Exchange.

"That certainly puts an end to my financial woes." Jim threw an apple in the air and caught it. "How about that? We finally hit the big time! I'll spread the good news to our field force." His first call was to his old college friend John Brown in San Jose.

Happy but calm, Fred's first call was to Peggy. "It's been a rough ride, but we're a public company, sweetheart; dust off your shopping list."

He then told his secretary to set up an employee cocktail hour to celebrate and to invite some of the nearby businesses to share their joy. The party was a roaring success.

Rick and Gloria joined in the celebration. Rick mentioned he was comfortable with his position at the law firm. Gloria had no further misgivings about stock being only pieces of paper. She told Rick she would use her credit card to spruce up their Eichler. She even talked to Rick about a bigger house for the family.

***

Fred and Rick took the Larkspur ferry into The City. The nearly empty ship had already shuttled the bulk of the commuters. Fred walked up to the food counter, looked over the fresh offerings, and selected hot coffee and several pastry items. He returned to their seats near the front window and placed his offering on the table between them. With a smile, Rick thanked him. Fred stubbed his Marlboro out in the ashtray alongside the armrest and selected a glazed doughnut.

"You've got to take time off. Come with me for a ride in my Crate 38," Fred said. "That little bi-wing stunt plane is my pride and joy. Ever since I stopped flying jets out of New Orleans with the reserves, I haven't gotten flying out of my blood. I have to admit I don't have much time to fly it. If I can get up in the air one or two weekends a month, it makes my hangar at Gnoss Field worthwhile."

Rick set his briefcase onto the adjacent seat. "I can empathize with that. But I've scratched my itch with *Snoopy,* my little Aeronca. She's an old high-winged, fabric-covered, two-place airplane with a propeller and a small sixty-five horsepower engine—like a Piper Cub from World War II and even earlier vintage. I can strap Ricky and Randy onto the backseat with one seat belt. I love cruising out over Bodega Bay and the coast at about 3,000 feet. Most of the time, it's just God and me up there."

"That's way too slow. My Crate 38 has two seats, just like yours, but that little red and white bi-plane of mine has get-up-and-go pizzazz. I can do acrobatics with it. I'm sure yours can't."

"You are right, but look at it this way. We're fortunate. We each have what we want to enjoy in our leisure time. And I can probably fly mine for a month without using up the gas you use on a single flight." Rick took a bite of a donut.

As their jet-powered ferry passed Alcatraz Island in San Francisco Bay, Rick looked out to the east. "Look at the beautiful sunrise lingering over the crowded Golden Gate Bridge."

"I'm sure glad we don't have to drive in that traffic every day. These ferries are much more comfortable. Look, you can see the Marin headlands reaching toward Mt Tamalpais."

"Inspiring," Rick replied.

***

Rick and Fred liked their new office at Wood Island. Rough-cut redwood paneled the conference room. A spacious and comfortable room became Rick's office when he worked there. For Rick, a peanut shop, like the one he used to use on Bush Street was the only thing missing.

The redwood building took up most of the island. On the ground floor, a large conference room with eight chairs gave the space a professional look. Full-sized basketball and racquetball courts helped the staff let off steam.

***

The recruiting net widened. The company needed a corporate airplane to facilitate recruiting and support the branch offices. Fred called Frank Gavin who knew John Carrigan, a Vice President at Cessna Aircraft Corporation.

"When John flies over here to Nashville in his Cessna 335, he usually stops in and visits. You know that the 335 is a little bigger than what you need right now, it seats six—two in the front and four behind. Both you and Rick are pilots, and so is Marco Flynn. It might be time for John Carrigan to trade his plane in for one of the new models."

"We don't have cash available right now for an airplane. Do you think John Carrigan might be interested in a private-stock-for-Cessna transaction?"

Frank said, "I'll find out whether he'd be interested in a meeting with you the next time he comes to the West Coast."

Later on, John Carrigan called Fred and told him of his interest in selling the Cessna for private stock. He said he would be in the Bay Area the following week, and he wanted to discuss the sale— he was amenable to Fred's offer of private stock for the airplane.

Fred told him the company's public stock had been trading in the range of $52 to $53 per share since the IPO. They agreed to exchange the airplane for private stock. John wanted $250,000 but admitted that the price was negotiable. Fred offered 4,800 non-registered American Financial shares at $50 per share; that amounted to a $240,000 for the plane. John Carrigan accepted the offer.

John said he would fly the Cessna to Gnoss Field in Novato on his trip to San Francisco next week. Fred and Rick were then checked out in the operation of the Cessna at that airport. Both men made take-offs and landings with John Carrigan and got answers to all of their questions. They were both pleased with the airplane.

Fred and John Carrigan signed the papers to exchange the airplane for American Financial private stock. The Cessna was taxied into the hangar at Gnoss Field that would be its new home. Marco Flynn ended up doing most of the flying for the company as he took Jim and others to their destinations as work required.

A lunchroom was at the east end of that hangar. The Cessna 335 had two pilot seats in the front, and four in the cabin behind the pilots. One pilot could easily fly the aircraft. The plane had a fuel tank at the end of each wing tip to provide extra distance when taking a long cross-country flight. There were two wing-tip gasoline tanks, which gave it additional range.

In February 1972, George Murphy, a Hollywood dancer and actor, ran for Senator in California. His people approached Fred to rent the Cessna so Mr. Murphy could use it on the campaign trail. Mr. Murphy's pilot was already checked out in a Cessna 335. Fred agreed to rent it to Mr. Murphy's campaign.

Landing at Gnoss Field late one night, the pilot parked the Cessna between the hangar and the airfield gas pumps. He then fueled both tip tanks, tied the plane down, and went to his motel room to sleep. He planned an early morning departure for campaigning the next day.

That night, two teenagers decided to rob the restaurant. They broke into the north end of the hangar. When they had what they wanted, they set a small fire in the restaurant to hide their fingerprints. The fire got out of control, and the boys fled. The east wall of the hangar burst into flames. The starboard fuel tip tank of the airplane, only a few feet from the burning wall, exploded, and the fire burned the entire right side of the Cessna.

The insurance policy contained a provision stating the plane must be hangared overnight. Parking it on the ramp, between the gas pumps near the hangar, wasn't good enough. The insurance company declined to pay for most of the damage. Rick's negotiations with the claims department went nowhere.

Jim was irate when he heard what had happened. "What the hell's is wrong with that pilot?" Jim growled. "He knew where he was supposed to park the damn thing."

Fred tried to assuage him. "Look at it this way, Jim. We didn't use our cash to buy the plane. We used our company's treasury stock; that's the only loss from the fire."

"That's a piss-poor excuse!"

The D.A. prosecuted, and the boys ended up in Juvenile Hall. The parents incurred a large debt but had little money. With Fred's urging, Mr.

Murphy contributed to the amount owed. "After all," Fred said, "it was Murphy's pilot who chose to park the aircraft outside the hangar near the gas pumps.

Marco later bought a smaller twin-engine Piper Aztec to replace the doomed Cessna. The Aztec, located at the nearby Napa Airport, only seated four, but the plane was comfortable with a range of 650 miles.

CHAPTER EIGHT

The Rewards

With the public offering of their common stock comfortably astern, Fred decided to take a break from the wild rides and long hours. He invited Marco, Rick, and their wives to join him and Peggy on a short vacation in southern Spain. Jim, off on a new campaign in the Inland Empire, didn't want to join them.

The trip started in Costa del Sol on the south coast of Spain. From there, they took a ferry to Algeciras to cross the Strait of Gibraltar and on to Morocco in northwest Africa.

Susan Flynn was happy to have Peggy Maloney, her old Pensacola friend, to talk with. Once they relaxed, Susan became comfortable sharing intimate details with Peggy.

"You can't imagine how difficult the last couple months with Marco have been," Susan started. "He's gone so much." She gazed into the distance. "I know he loves me, and that Fred keeps him swamped. But he's got a roving eye." She shook her head. "I can't trust him anymore."

"I know you think Marco fools around," Peggy replied. "But I don't. I'm sure Jim and others are, but from what little I have seen of Marco, I think he just likes to look."

Tears welled in Sue's eyes. "Do you *really* think so? I know he acts like he loves me when he's home, but he does so much traveling. God, it would be wonderful if you were right."

"Well, I can't be sure. But I have watched a lot of men come and go. You get a feel for who's running around. I don't think Marco is one of them."

Susan wiped her red eyes with her shawl. "He works so hard, and I love him so much."

Grateful for Peggy's support, Susan felt comforted. She wiped the few tears from her eyes and put her arm around Peggy. As they approached the African shore, they rejoined the rest of the group.

***

After they arrived at Marrakesh in Morocco, everyone walked to Jemaa el-Fnaa in the Medina quarter of Marrakesh. Tourists filled the marketplace courtyard and mixed with the locals. The snake charmer fascinated the ladies. He sat cross-legged in front of a basket and played his flute. As if by magic, the cobra lifted from its coiled position—hood spread and seemingly ready to bite. The women jumped back, but instead of lunging, the mesmerized snake swayed to the tune.

And next, the camel. The ladies refused to have their pictures taken on its back.

"What if the camel spits?" Gloria said with distaste.

"Camels rarely spit," the handler replied.

The women shook their heads. The snake charmer was enough excitement for one day.

An Arab took care of the two camels on duty that afternoon. A third Arab accepted coins and paper money from those waiting for their turn.

When the camel kneeled, its rider disembarked, and the next patron climbed into the seat. The camel stood up to its full height, legs straight, and faced the remaining Arab who gingerly held his Voigtlander camera and captured the passengers' smiling faces on film. Their pictures would be ready at the gate later in the afternoon.

In the hot sun, the crowd thinned, and the camels took a break from doing their daily push-ups. Curious, Peggy stepped toward a resting camel, its knees tucked under its body. Up close, the camel was beautiful with his long legs, arching back, and a long snout, but its bad breath caused her to step back, her face squinched from disgust.

While the men explored the rest of the marketplace, the women surveyed stands laden with Moroccan clothing and souvenirs. A tall, dark Arab, wrapped in a tattered blanket spoke Arabic with a smattering of broken English, offered his goods to passersby.

A colorful blouse caught Peggy's eye, and she headed toward the vendor. The Arab held up five fingers, smiled, and muttered something in Arabic.

Peggy shook her head, held up one finger, and said, "One dollar."

He frowned, talked to himself a moment, and dropped his bid to four fingers.

Peggy shook her head with vigor. She handed the blouse back to him and held up two fingers.

With three fingers held high, the Arab countered.

Peggy showed him two American dollars, which the Arab took and handed her the blouse. She smiled, gave the other women a thumbs up, and dropped the festive shirt into her bag.

The Arab looked at Peggy. "Where ya from?" he said in clear unbroken English.

Stunned, Peggy turned to face him. "Excuse me?"

"Where are you from," the Arab said, this time with a wink.

Peggy couldn't help but laugh. "San Francisco."

"I went to San Francisco State," he said with a wide grin.

When the men returned Gloria and Susan were laughing. Susan, looking happier than she'd been in a long time, waved them over. After a lively conversation, the couples boarded the ferry to return to Spain.

***

When he got back to California, Rick went right to work. On his way home from his office at Woodford and Hoskins, Rick headed north from San Francisco on Highway 101. Rick savored the sunset as it thrust its fading yellow and orange rays across the Farallon Islands and toward the ocean west of the Golden Gate Bridge. Lost in thoughts of times he'd spent in Marrakesh with the Navy in 1954, Rick drove past the exit to his home in lower Lucas Valley. When he realized he'd gone too far, he didn't care. The beauty of the green hills flowing, poppies bursting into bloom, and the horses grazing brought him a sense inner of peace. An occasional ranch house appeared.

As he slowed to make a U-turn to head home, he spotted a For Sale sign on the south side of the road. Rick pulled over and climbed from his car. Sixteen Acres! A diagram defined the perimeter of the property and the various structures.

Up the hill, at the end a circular driveway, a sprawling ranch house sat. Five bedrooms and a flagstone swimming pool. The living and the dining room shared a flagstone fireplace, and off of there was another room for an office. Three *bedrooms could be used for the girls. Later on, we could convert the attached three-car carport into another bedroom for the twins.*

At the top of the property, a small lake beckoned. The sixteen acres provided a natural playground with plenty of room for the girls to raise horses. Becky and Jody could practice in the riding ring and show their quarter horses. The twins could care for chickens and sell eggs to neighbors around upper Lucas Valley. Best of all, Rick could enjoy fishing at the lake.

He squinted to read the sign in the fading light. A large metal barn sat on the west side of the property near the neighbor's driveway that continued up the hill towards the small lake at the top of the hill. On the east side of the property, another barn, made from rustic redwood, sat near an adjacent redwood fenced riding ring. The redwood barn had four horse stalls and a feeding area for horses. Tall prairie grass grew in the center of the riding ring.

This property is where dreams come to life. The girls, always thrilled to help their girlfriends with their horses, loved brushing the majestic creatures. What a fantastic place for them to grow up. When the boys get a little bigger, I'm sure they will like horses too.

As he drove back down Lucas Valley Road, he worried. How can I explain this to Gloria? *We don't have much cash, and I can't sell company stock right now—-as an insider at American Financial, my sale of stock is restricted for the first two years following our IPO. But I could use our stock as extra collateral for a promissory note if Dr. Malone, the neighbor to the east who owned the property, would accept a five year note as part of the purchase price.*

When he walked through his front door, he gave Gloria a kiss and a smile. "Where are the children?"

"Becky's on a sleepover," Gloria replied. "The boys are in bed. Jody and Sue are upstairs doing homework."

Rick breathed a sigh of relief. "I just found the place we've been looking to purchase. A stable to keep horses for the girls. A swimming pool on the back patio. A lake for fishing." He laid his briefcase on the dining room table, pulled out a yellow pad, and retrieved his Cross pencil from his shirt pocket. "Honey, you're not going to believe this," he said.

Rick had transcribed everything he'd seen on the For Sale sign onto his yellow pad. When Gloria went over it with Fred, her eyes grew wide. Rick wasn't sure whether he saw tears of sorrow or joy.

"We can't afford something like that," she spouted. "It would be wonderful for the children, and I'm sure the two of us would love all the views. But it's out of the question, especially with you gone all the time. And the boys don't even know how to swim yet. I'm not moving to a ranch with a pool until you teach the twins how to swim."

After negotiating with the neighbor, Dr. Malone, Rick made a deal work by giving him a five-year note secured by American Financial stock. Rick promised Gloria he'd take enough time off from work to teach both boys how to swim.

Gloria stuck to her point: stock differs from cash. "You can't pay that note off with stock," she told Rick. "Why don't you take all your stock, sell it, and put the cash on the dining room table where I can see it. Then you can take that cash and repurchase your stock."

Rick knew she was being cute. She already knew he couldn't sell it because of his relationship with the company. But when all was said and done, the Taylors decided to purchase the ranch.

Rick fell in love with the property. Gloria, although not as enthused, could see the girls were happy. Their focus on caring for the horses impressed her. And the boys had learned to swim—with their life jackets on and zipped up in the back.

But what about that five-year promissory note? He didn't want to sell their stock, even though it had a good run-up. He thought five years was a good time to wait before he sold some of the stock. However, Gloria's fears about that five-year promissory note hung over her like a guillotine.

"It won't do you much good to sit and worry about something five years away," Rick told her.

She gave up worrying about paying for the ranch, yet in the back of her mind, doubts still lingered.

One day, Jody and Becky watched the vet nailing horseshoes.

"I expect you'll have a new foal soon."

Becky said, "*Really*? When will the new foal come?"

He told the girls to keep an eye on the mare's nipples. "When wax forms, the foal will be ready to be born."

Their eyes widened. A quizzical expression crossed Jody's face. She wasn't yet old enough to be familiar with all the parts of the horse.

When Rick heard that Predawn was pregnant, he nailed boards around the three-car carport and spread dry straw on the ground. The carport was now a horse stall, fenced in for the mare while she awaited the birth.

Each of the three girls invited two friends to watch Predawn give birth. Each day, when the girls came home from school, they would go to Predawns's stall and check her nipples.

Peggy and her bridge group turned heads when Becky and Jody came charging through the door shouting, "She has wax on her nipples! She has wax on her nipples!" That gave the bridge group pause. The two girls ran back out the door to let their friends know today was the day.

A little after nine that evening, the three girls and six friends surrounded the mare. With arms hung over the wooden boards outside the carport, they waited. Soon, two small front legs dropped out of the horse with what looked like saran wrap hanging below them. Next, a slender brown head appeared between those two front legs, and the birth continued. The foal, already named Barney, fell to the ground, staggered to stand up, fell, got up, and finally stood on wobbly legs. Each child had a different facial reaction—amazement, fascination, nausea, elation—the full gamut.

Rick wished he could use light for a photo, but he didn't want to scare Predawn while she gave birth. Since Dr. Peterson didn't make it in time, Rick was glad he had prepared for Barney's birth by researching everything he could find on pregnant horses.

***

When Fred heard about Predawn, he phoned Rick. "Hello Dr. Taylor, this is Fred Maloney. We have a black lab that's about to give birth, and I heard you . . ." Fred laughed. "Rick! What the hell's going on at the Taylor ranch? I didn't know attorneys had so many talents."

When the laughing subsided, Rick asked, "What's up?"

"I want to get a golf game together at the Meadow Club on Saturday. Any chance you can tear yourself away from birthing and join Keith, Pat Raab, and me?"

"Love to Fred, but I promised next Saturday to Gloria and the kids. I owe her one from the Nashville trip at New Year's."

Fred understood. He then called Bart Haas, an attorney friend who lived near Fred in Greenbrae.

The foursome took the first tee at the Meadow Club at noon on Saturday. It was a perfect day for golf. Fred led off and delivered his ball straight down the fairway. It landed thirty-two yards shy of the green. Pat's ball landed about eighteen yards short of Fred's. Keith and Bart both stayed in the fairway, near Pat's ball.

After they closed out the sixteenth hole and headed for the seventeenth tee, Pat invited Fred to join him at one of his golf clubs in Palm Springs. Pat had two houses in the Palm Springs area. Planning for his retirement at the bank, Pat told

Fred he didn't want to worry about both of those houses while he continued to live in Kentfield.

"I love Palm Springs. I would love to get a place down there. Peggy and I could use it some during January and February and rent it out for the rest of the year. Now that the kids are older, a place in Palm Springs could motivate Peggy to get back on the golf course." Fred thought a moment and then continued. "If you don't need the cash right away, we could put together a contract so I could rent it from you for a few years—until my restriction on selling my stock is lifted. Then, I could either give you some of my stock or sell it and pay you in cash for the house. Which one of the places would you be selling?"

"If you're serious Fred, I could sell you the one at the Indian Canyons Golf Resort in Palm Springs and keep the other one and my home here in Marin."

"Yes, I am serious.

"Let me give it some thought. I'll work on the numbers."

The transaction turned into a perfect fit. Bart Haas put the paperwork together for his two friends. Both wives weighed in, and the deal closed. It was October 1972.

***

On April 4, 1973, a crowd gathered around the TV in the American Financial employee lounge at Wood Island.

"What's going on?" Fred asked as he approached the group.

"You won't believe it! ABC TV news just announced that Equity Funding Corporation of America has been shut down by the California Insurance Commissioner for accounting fraud and the use of a computer to maintain fictitious life insurance policies. The reporter said 100 company employees deceived investors, auditors, reinsurers, and regulatory authorities."

"Holy shit." Fred couldn't believe it.

Equity Funding clerks had issued life insurance policies on deceased people. This had been going on for an extended period. Everyone was in shock. Fred's employees wondered what the impact would be on American Financial, the only other company that offered funding. They had often heard how the rising stock of Equity Funding was a catalyst for the stock of American Financial Planning Corporation.

Fraud charges were brought against the Equity Funding Corporation of America. Twenty-two individuals pleaded guilty or were convicted. Investigators found six hundred bogus life insurance policies, and the company's president and executive vice president went to jail. One report said Equity Funding, raking in two billion dollars, was the most prominent U.S. swindle in the 200-year history of the country. Equity Funding was no longer in business.

Speechless when he first heard the news, Jim said, "Well, that explains why it was so hard to understand how Equity Funding could report such great financial numbers. We've been winning the battle against almost every Equity Funding office we've competed with, yet they kept winning on Wall Street with their stock."

Bud Johnson added, "They even fooled sophisticated investors. Duped Major Wall Street banks. The life insurance premium volume they reported simply did not exist."

"Wow," Jim said. "This will be a major story in *The Wall Street Journal*."

"It will be over all the front pages across the country," Fred added.

And it was. News reports continued to expand. Equity Funding coverage went full force for several weeks. Described as "the financial crisis of the twentieth century," the scandal was a colossus crime supported by computer systems. Regulatory investigations continued over many months.

The fraud began in 1964 with a fictitious annual report. The CEO of Equity Funding ordered fabricated accounting entries to meet the regulatory filing deadline. A scheme had been put in place to inflate financial statements through the creation of nonexistent insurance and other bogus assets.

Equity Funding Corporation of America, once the darling of institutional investors, sold millions of dollars of fraudulent life insurance policies. Forged bonds and certificates of deposit inflated the assets of the company and its subsidiary. Illegal insider trading occurred before reports of widespread financial irregularities became public knowledge.

Institutional investors dumped huge blocks of the stock. Brokerage firms, banks, and other institutions suffered heavy losses. Many filed lawsuits against Equity Funding's officers, accountants, reinsurers, and lawyers.

A lawsuit claimed that one stockbroker handled stock transactions for "insiders," and split the profits with them. Equity Funding Corporation sold hundreds of millions of dollars of phantom life insurance policies with premiums totaling millions of dollars. In California, twenty million dollars of bonds, issued to support insurance premiums, did not exist.

Senior employees of Equity Funding had created phony insurance policies on company computers to back up their false entries. Equity Funding then reinsured these fake policies with several other insurers. They also faked the deaths of some of these nonexistent individuals and took the death benefits into Equity Funding.

Prosecutors charged twenty-two individuals and estimated that fifty others at the company knew of the fraud. In 1973, a disgruntled ex-employee had reported the scheme to a Wall Street analyst who covered the insurance industry. That analyst then discussed the company with his clients, many of whom sold Equity Funding stock before the fraud became public knowledge. The Equity Funding cases helped to establish a new legal precedent regarding insider trading.

The Equity Funding scandal—considered the first computer-based fraud—created phony documents to back up the false policies. It became so cumbersome that Equity Funding Corporation of America used computers to automate the deception. (The first news report, by *The New York Times*, is reproduced in the Postscript.)

ACT III
Buckle Up

CHAPTER NINE
Finding a New Way

When Fred Maloney heard about the news reports of Equity Funding Corporation of America, he called Peggy. He told her that there had been some bad news at the office, and he would explain it to her later. He would be late for supper, he said, but they could talk about it when he got home.

Peggy threw two logs into the fireplace for Fred to light when he arrived. It was late when he walked in. Fred looked tired and disheveled. Peggy poured coffee into Fred's cup as he hung up his coat. "When did you last eat?"

"Doesn't matter. I'm exhausted, but I'm not hungry." Fred headed to the sofa, sat down, and took a sip of his coffee. "Jim has always had his suspicions about Equity Funding's claims of life insurance production. I didn't disagree with him, but I sure didn't expect this."

Peggy wondered what was going on. She pulled out Fred's favorite pecan pie, cut a slice for him, and brought it into the living room. "Bring me up to date."

"Honey, we've spent a lot of time and treasure getting Forrest to approve funding for Pioneer Life. The television reports say that Equity Funding has been shut down for recording fictitious life insurance sales. Equity's funding crimes will have our sales force in a panic. They won't want to even talk about funding anymore."

Fred took a bite of the pie and offered some to Peggy.

"This is really going to hurt us, honey, no matter how it washes out. We can't offer life insurance policies with funding for now—maybe never. Some things are never forgotten. Unfortunately, fear hangs on like a damn tick on a stray dog."

"What about the Palm Springs house? We've barely gotten it ready to rent," she said quietly.

Fred shook his head and shrugged.

Peggy tried, but couldn't console Fred. She pulled her chair closer to his, rubbed his back, stroked his arm, and reached for his hand. Her eyes filled with tears.

Fred walked to the fireplace and lit the logs. They talked for the better part of an hour. Fred said he had to get into the office early, and they went to bed.

As Fred fiddled with his pillow, he noticed Peggy had fallen asleep. But for him, the restlessness he felt kept him tossing and turning. Had he gone too far? Maybe he should have paid more attention to Jim and focused on life insurance sales. Had he put too much emphasis on funding?

Without funding would they lose Jim? If so, the force of Jim's absence would devastate American Financial. Would Jim drop Pioneer Life and return to West Coast Life? That would leave the company in a lurch. These questions swirled in his mind. It was hard to sleep.

He learned in the Marine Corps that when the going gets tough, the tough get going. *What have I done? After all this work, have I set us up for a fall? No. I must pick myself up from the gravel and keep moving.*

***

When Fred stepped through the door at the office the next morning, all the employees sat, waiting. His mouth was parched; his stomach hollowed. General anxiety rolled through him to create a discomfort he rarely felt.

"We'll probably have to give up funding because the funding part of Equity's fraud will attach to our company, even though American Financial has done no wrong." *It's human nature.*

"American Financial is a viable company, and you shouldn't fear for your jobs," Fred offered. Only a small part of the company is involved in funding—it's a new product for us. You've all done excellent jobs at serving customers, and the condemnation of funding will not influence the myriad of other financial products we offer." Fred hesitated and surveyed the faces of the employees. "I hope I still have your support and loyalty." He could see in their eyes and demeanor that he could hold this company together through the tragedy. He knew they were up to the task.

After the meeting, Fred stood alone in his office, hands in his pants pockets, his cigarette smoldering in the nearby ashtray. He considered the countless phone calls he received the night before and this morning. The sales force had to know how to handle the Equity Funding scandal.

Fred gazed down the Greenbrae channel toward the Richmond Bridge. He reminisced about the sailing weekends he spent on the Bay and flying over the whole the area in his Crate 38. Fred's love of flying had never left him. But today, the daydreaming didn't distract him.

Life couldn't always be the way he planned it. He had to deal with reality. The good alternatives outweighed the crisis, and his goal of financial planning for the common man was still alive. There was no way to avoid being tainted by the murky

Equity Funding brush. Even so, Fred couldn't turn away from the financial planning idea he had nurtured for so long. He decided to continue forward. He had an army, and he would make sure his army was well fed.

He put his Marlboro out in the ashtray, tightened his belt, and answered the ringing telephone, again.

He asked his trusted secretary to take most calls and headed to the conference room. Surrounded in silence, Fred and Bud Johnson waited for Jim and Rick to arrive. Fred also invited his advisory committee and hoped some of them could make the meeting on such short notice. Fred's secretary placed water, coffee cups, and napkins around the table. When the others came in, she offered them water and coffee.

Jim and Rick pulled their chairs up to the conference table. Jim wore a scowl on his face and didn't even say good morning to the group. Bud, seated at the other end of the table, sat with his shoulders drooped, his eyes focused on the thick carpet. Rick greeted them and sat down next to Fred.

The atmosphere was taut—no one uttered a word as they settled around the table. It was time to talk about new ideas. Make new plans. Fred started.

"I haven't come up with anything new, fellas. Looks to me like we are *de facto* out of the funding business for the foreseeable future—maybe forever.

There are so many twists and turns in these news reports. Separating fact from fiction is difficult, but the huge financial fraud is real. We have to turn to the advantages of financial planning for the middle class and be careful to maintain our good reputation with the regulators *and* our customers."

They all agreed to focus on traditional recruiting tactics to find new insurance agents and mutual fund reps, their new lifeblood. They were now grateful that back in the Palace Hotel days they hadn't chosen to name their new company Capital Funding Corporation.

Rick Taylor said, "It's pretty early to tell, but the fraud in their system is a fact. I can't see how we can live with funding as a product or as a service either—at least until all the facts are known. We can spend all day arguing that we are not Equity Funding, but this fraud is just too big to ignore.

"We have to shift our focus, and our branch office leadership, away from funding—at least for a while." Rick took a sip of coffee. "Setting a new corporate goal that lands between financial planning and delivering traditional investment products is smart. We must move forward as a credible financial conglomerate offering traditional financial services, and add some additional products for our field force."

"I'm fed up with it—*fed up with it*," Jim spewed. "All the guys want to know is whether we'll still offer funding. Well, we can't do that. We set up our new funding operation, and it works. The Golden Gate Securities Company staff handles it very well. We're within the law, but I agree that we have to change course."

Fred thought about it. "We must continue to administer those Pioneer Life policies sold with funding. If a policyholder wants a different policy, we need to make it easy for him to get out and choose a new policy. Let's get Pioneer Life's actuaries busy on a replacement life insurance policy we can live with—and know the customer will be comfortable with."

Bud said, "I'll work with the actuaries and with David Walsh & Company to do the best we can to make sure that the customer doesn't get hurt in the process—even if it means we'll have losses."

Fred agreed. "I think Bud's correct. We've got to protect our customers and move on. We do well in mutual fund and life insurance sales, and we need to concentrate on both."

Jim ranted on. "Without the advantage of funding, we are just another conglomerate selling life insurance and mutual funds. I'm fed up with it."

Astounded, Fred replied, "What the hell are you talking about, Jim?"

"I agree that American Financial must bring on other financial products. But I'll stay with what I know best—recruiting life insurance salesmen. Some recruits won't buy Pioneer Life, but I can still sell them West Coast Life."

Fred felt a wave of heat move from his neck to his face. He gritted his teeth and clenched his fists to restrain from lunging at Jim and shaking sense into him.

"We don't need that kind of mindset to go forward." Ignoring Jim, Fred turned to the others. "We have to distinguish American Financial from the torrent of bad news about Equity Funding. American Financial Planning Corporation needs a new direction. ASAP. We're a conglomerate with various subsidiaries delivering different financial products and advice. Emphasize that we are a *financial* company. That does not include funding anymore, but we still have a clear path to financial planning among our products."

"Our stock dropped back to thirty-one dollars a share in less than a week—half of last week's price," Bud said. "It's been oscillating between 30 and 33 dollars a share today. This scandal is a disaster that no one could have

226

foreseen. It's time to make sure that American Financial doesn't get painted with the same dirty brush as Equity Funding. We need a new business plan."

Bud added, "An accountant friend of mine in Monterey bought a new boat for his family when our stock continued to grow after the IPO. And one of Karen's girlfriends went ahead with a facial operation she didn't think she could afford."

Fred chipped in, "Yeah. And that's about when I bought Crate 38."

Jim looked at Rick, who sat at the other end of the table. "And you didn't waste any time either, Rick," Sarcasm lined his words. "You bought that horse trailer for your ranch. I don't know why you thought those girls of yours needed more practice, considering all the blue ribbons they've already won.

***

Later on, Fred's advisory committee assembled in the second-floor conference room at Wood Island, a relaxed setting where they could take time to come up with plans to redefine the company and get it moving again.

Fred started the discussion. "Let's talk about how we can regroup and live with the negative publicity Equity Funding has left for us."

As the men continued to be seated around the conference table, Fred continued, "It's ironic— just two months ago our subsidiary, Golden Gate Securities Company, received an award for quality from the National Association of Securities Dealers (NASD)."

"I feel comfortable with the sales force we have assembled," Jim said. "I believe that the current insurance and mutual fund production will continue to increase . . . when the initial shock wears off."

The mood in the conference room lightened when they heard Jim talking; they wanted to share his optimism. It had been only two weeks since the crisis, and new life insurance sales only showed a small decline. Keith Raab had flown in to talk with Fred. He joined the men at the table. It was easy to see why he'd gone far with the Strategic Air

Command. His presence alone commanded attention. Sitting tall, as though still in uniform, he had the authority his extensive business experience had given him since leaving the Air Force.

"There's no way to convince the public that funding is beneficial rather than wrong or illegal—not after the great Equity Funding Corporation of America financial fraud," Keith said. "American Financial will be like a fish swimming upstream against the current, and the company will spend plenty of time trying to convince consumers *our* funding isn't a problem." Keith shook his head. "We have to drop funding—immediately."

Marco Flynn had also flown in from Pensacola to join the Wood Island meeting. He was sure the stigma would not leave the national news reports soon. "You can bank on that."

Frank Gavin was firm on his opinion that the company must stand on its merit and that it needed to publicize its advantages, not just complain about Equity Funding.

Frank felt discouraged. "This fiasco has been hell on Nashville Life. We were just getting geared up for funding when the shit hit the fan. Funding is new with American Financial; life insurance and mutual funds have been around for a long time. Separating ourselves from Equity Funding won't be enough. We have to spend as much money as needed to tell our own story, funding not included."

He advocated heavy advertising with quality national magazines and life insurance associations. "I don't think we can move the needle with only the approval of our friends and business associates."

Fred put his cigarette out and stood up. "I agree with Frank. Separating ourselves from Equity Funding isn't enough. We have to emphasize our positives. We need to talk about the financial products and services we provide to the public. Frank has identified a good place to start—get the media on our side through advertising."

The advisory committee settled on actively detailing the history and quality of American Financial with heavy advertising rather than trying to contrast the company from the fraud of Equity Funding Corporation.

"It is going to be difficult for the rest of 1973," Marco said.

"We have to haul in the lines and tack into these headwinds," Fred replied.

Frank Gavin added, "Our best defense is a smart offense. We need to understand who in the financial services industry is on our side and ask them for help. I don't think Fred's talk about financial planning has burned any bridges. We have friends out there, like United Express Company. Let's get our story out to the public and avoid criticizing Equity Funding."

Marco volunteered to accept the publicity task. He would call on *Business Week, Time, Look,* and *The Saturday Evening Post* to see what help he could get. Marco ultimately convinced several of those news editors, especially the editor from *Time* magazine, to review the company's production reports and history in the financial services industry with him. Marco also helped produce media copy for local advertising in large cities.

The favorable news stories helped. The American Financial stock price overcame the initial shock of the Equity Funding news and began a slow move toward its pre-crisis level. It took a while, but the stock price grew, sparked by the company's positive quarterly 10-Q financial report to the SEC and filings with the State of California.

After the others left the meeting, Fred thought more about the mindset of his agents and reps, and told Jim "More products are needed if we want recruits in this environment,"

"I've got a new product idea," Jim said.

"Let's get together at the Meadow Club this afternoon. I have a golf game scheduled with Phil Schmidt and two of his men. After that, you and I can take our time to go over your idea," offered Fred.

CHAPTER TEN
Becoming a Conglomerate

The Meadow Club, a short drive from San Francisco to Marin County, was the first golf course in North America designed by Alister MacKenzie in 1925. Members were proud of their heritage. Fred hadn't been playing much golf recently, but it was his favorite place to meet and greet prospects.

Jim found a chair on the expansive redwood deck overlooking the eighteenth fairway. He watched Fred putt his ball into the cup, shake hands with his golfing partners, and excuse himself from the foursome. Fred then walked up the hill to the clubhouse, found Jim, and they selected chairs at an empty table.

"As we keep growing, new product development gets tougher," Jim began.

"I know. What do you have in mind?" Fred pulled out a cigarette and settled in his chair. Always in control, Fred had weathered the fallout from the Equity Funding crisis well.

"Our customers know they should provide for their long-term care," Jim said. "But most people either think long-term care is too far down the road for them to worry about or that Alzheimer's or dementia won't happen to them. Besides, they believe that long-term care insurance premiums will keep rising, and that the coverage doesn't go far enough to protect them against all the costs. Procrastination leaves the clients to do the best they can do for their future. They would rather purchase a fixed annuity to provide them with a guaranteed income in their later years."

"Ok. So, we sell annuities. Where are you going with this?"

"Those few agents who do sell long-term care insurance put it with Transamerica Insurance Company, Fred. I've been working with Transamerica for a long time. Their actuary and I used to play handball together."

"I'm familiar with Transamerica's long-term care product," Fred replied. "I get it. We sell life insurance, long-term care policies, and annuities. It would be a real winner if we could link them all together. Long-term care policies get a good reception right now. Combining the three products would certainly be unique. I'll talk to CEO Roger Williams and see if he's willing to consider a new type of policy that combines life insurance, annuities, and long-term care protection into a single insurance policy."

"You've got it." Jim picked up the tempo. "Then, if the policyholder remains healthy and decides he won't need the insurance, the policy could either pay a death benefit or provide an annuity—at the discretion of the client."

Fred put his cigarette out in the ashtray, and looked at Jim. "Hmm. Your idea has merit, Jim. So, upon reaching the normal retirement age of 65, the customer can make a decision based on his assessment of his health and finances at that time."

"Roger's actuaries would decide how to structure the policy, whether it's an election or a default trigger," Jim replied.

The following Thursday, Fred made a full presentation of his plan to Roger Williams and his staff at the Transamerica Pyramid.

"We'll put our actuaries to work on the project and see what they come up with," Roger told Fred. "I'll get back to you by the end of the month. From a marketing point of view, it's a good idea, but we have to see what the actuaries say."

***

On his way home from the Meadow Club, Fred thought about his old friend, Bob Green in Wisconsin. Bob and Fred had known each other ever since the two were first licensed to sell life insurance. When Fred was still in Florida, he always followed Bob's exceptional life insurance production from afar. They kept in touch over the years.

From their homes in Milwaukee, Bob Green and his partner, Eric Steinberg, had been selling life insurance throughout the Midwest for a long time.

Bob knew about Fred's interest in funding, but neither he nor Eric ever wanted to get involved with it. They chose not to rock the boat. Many of their agents and reps who sold life insurance also sold mutual funds.

"Bob Green is an old friend of mine," Fred told Jim. "He and his partner, Eric Steinberg, are wholesalers for General Electric's life insurance company. They recruit agents from all over the Midwest, and from the South.

"I know Bob has kept his eye on American Financial for a long time. He and I have known each other ever since I started selling life insurance. I've talked to Bob about financial planning, but he wants to stay with life insurance. I want to see if we can develop some life insurance business with them. I'll see how Bob feels about Equity Funding."

"Better be careful with that one," Rick cautioned. "If General Electric has them under contract, they won't like Bob and Eric helping us."

"No guts, no air medal," Fred replied. "All Bob and Eric have to do is say 'no.' Whatever relationship they have with GE is up to them to figure out. I'll call Bob. I know he's always had an eye on moving away from the snow."

Bob Green told Fred that he never liked the idea of funding. "All this funding stuff is too complicated. But now that you mention it, Eric and I have been thinking about moving to California for the last year or so. Most of our kids are either in college or on their way. Two of mine are at Berkeley, and Eric has one that wants a degree from Cal Poly. This could be a good time to move."

Fred was encouraged. Bob didn't reject the idea of working with Fred; he just needed a catalyst.

"These guys are by far the leading life insurance producers for General Electric," Fred told Jim. "I understand the two of them make more money than the president of the GE life company. I've been keeping Bob up to date on what we're doing."

Fred invited Bob Green to stay at his house in Greenbrae for a couple of days. "Bring Pat along with you—we have plenty of room, and it will give her a chance to meet Peggy and get the lay of the land."

***

When the Greens came to Marin County, Pat fell in love with the marvelous home Fred and Peggy enjoyed. Pat did not bring up the subject of costs while she and Bob were in Marin. When Peggy asked Fred why, he told her, "Bob has made a lot of money with GE Life over the years. I don't think costs are much of a concern."

Bob Green toured the North Bay with Fred for two days and met some of Fred's managers and salesmen.

"Fred, it's encouraging to see how your men are following your advice in an unhappy situation. I thought the bad news about funding would dishearten them. You guys are doing a good job of handling things in this uncomfortable situation."

"Thanks. It has been a rough row to hoe. But no one has talked to Jim or me about leaving."

At the end of the week, Eric Steinberg and Bob Green met with Fred at Wood Island. Eric's wife chose not to come to California, even though there was plenty of room at the Maloney house for all. While they relaxed on the patio in the sunshine,

Fred talked with both men about the opportunities he saw for them in California. They would need a new source of life insurance, and Fred went into detail about Pioneer Life.

On the way to the San Francisco Airport on Monday, Fred drove Bob, Pat, and Eric across the Golden Gate Bridge to meet Phil Schmidt in San Francisco.

"If we decided to leave GE, it would have no connection to the Equity Funding crisis," Bob assured Fred. "We just aren't getting the attention from GE that we're used to—kind of like an old shoe."

Eric agreed. "That doesn't mean we planned to move out here. I think we are just into too much of a routine, and the company takes us for granted. Besides, there are plenty of territories to cover in the Midwest."

Bob jumped in. "But I've had my eye on California, too. As I told Fred, some of my kids talk about going to school out here. Eric and I didn't think about working with American Financial and funding. Our well-worn recruiting format works well for us no matter where we live. Tell us a little more about the Pioneer Life product line."

"Pioneer Life is based in Hartford," Fred said. "I think they would fit your needs well. It's competitive and highly rated. You'll be satisfied with it." Fred noticed no signs of resistance on either of their faces. "I think you should put your licenses with Pioneer Life. I'm not sure if they are licensed in all the states where you have agents, but there is plenty of room in the West."

California did not favor non-compete employment contracts. The producer contracts that Bob and Eric had with General Electric's life insurance company had run for so long, they had expired. This left them on a day-to-day or month-to-month contract. When they notified GE of their departure, the two men met stiff resistance. The original agreement, though expired, contained vesting provisions. Bob and Eric would continue to receive overwrite commissions from business written by agents they had recruited.

When they got back to Wisconsin, Bob called Fred. "We had a long talk on the plane.

We're going to see how our wives feel about a move out there. Pioneer Life looks good to both of us. We'll talk about it and get back to you."

They made the move. Bob and Eric continued with their specialty: find an agent, recruit him, and service the agent. They didn't care about getting involved with mutual funds. They wanted to stay with their proven marketing strategy. It had served them well over the years. Soon they recruited in Northern California with positive results and moved on to outlying areas in California. American Financial's life insurance business grew.

Fred introduced Bob and Eric to a lawyer friend of his, Bart Haas, who has defended litigation involving enforcement of noncompete clauses in contracts, restraint of trade, and restrictions against unfair competition in employment law. California did not favor non-compete contracts. Bart Haas sued General Electric and its life insurance subsidiary on behalf of Bob and Eric in San Francisco. Following lengthy negotiations, the lawsuit settled, and Bob and Eric could work for whomever they chose. Each man received a substantial financial settlement from General Electric.

Bob Green bought a new car with the letters "Merci GE" on the California license plate. American Financial felt much the same way. Bob purchased a home at the Marin Country Club in Novato. Eric bought a summer home on the north shore of Lake Tahoe. Eric and Bob established an annual poker party at Eric's new home at Lake Tahoe—silver dollars were made available to guests for use as poker chips.

***

Long-term capital, the issue that had taken so much of his time in the past, worried Fred. He took down money from his line of credit at the Wells Fargo Bank and loaned it to the company for working capital. The advertising campaign had also put a strain on the company's cash flow. New life insurance production from Bob and Eric helped.

"I know we haven't heard from Transamerica," Jim told Fred. "But I think it's time to introduce limited partnerships. My friend, Marty

Cohen, puts them together. Bud Johnson has been working with Marty, integrating two of his limited partnerships into Golden Gate Securities Company for sale by our reps. Our securities reps are selling a lot of mutual funds and a few limited partnerships. Their securities licenses permit reps to sell both products. The customer buys limited partnership interests, not partnership common stock, and gets steady income and tax deductions as a limited partner of the partnership."

Jim continued "Marty Cohen, or one of his business associates, serves as the general partner and he'll assume liabilities for partnership activity; the limited partners have no responsibility for what the partnership does, but they get a percentage of its income.

There are good commissions associated with those partnerships, Fred, and when we sell them, we make good money. As a real estate broker, Marty formed Cohen & Company about eight years ago in Long Beach. He's involved in land sales, shopping center development, and handles the buying and selling of commercial real estate. Marty wants to develop more limited partnerships. He has the capacity, but he needs a broker-dealer to sell limited partnership interests. I told him we would look at it. He could be a great addition to our team."

"I want to meet him," Fred said. He took one final puff and crushed the rest of his cigarette in the ashtray.

Marco Flynn ran a background check on Marty Cohen and his company. It came out clean. Fred then met with Marty at his office in Long Beach. Fred liked the aggressiveness he sensed in Marty. He was perceptive and astute in finance and had put a lot of effort into building up Cohen & Company for real estate brokerage.

"Business is good," Marty boasted. "I'd like to join you and Jim, but I want to be a stockholder, not just another employee. We're a small regional company in the Los Angeles area that can become a national company if we keep going. Jim has convinced me we could achieve that goal by linking up with you. But I want to continue to run the real estate business with my team."

"I know how you feel," Fred told Marty. "I have the same seeds you do, and I understand where you are going. We could work well together. I want to purchase your company and leave you in control of operating it. You would continue to be the president of Cohen & Company—we wouldn't even have to change the name. I've talked to Rick Taylor. We could write a provision that states you could keep control of Cohen & Company, and repurchase it if another company buys American Financial."

"That sounds doable," Marty said. "I'll have my attorney meet with Rick to work out the details."

"Great! I understand how you prize your ownership and don't want to accept an outright acquisition. I think we can work that out in the purchase agreement. Meanwhile, American Financial will consolidate the revenue of Cohen & Company into our income statement,"

Marty Cohen agreed. He extended his right hand. Fred clasped the outstretched palm and smiled. Deal!

***

The volume of mutual fund shares and life insurance sales, both from agents of the company and new agents recruited by Bob & Eric, produced additional income for American Financial. Fred thought about creating a small life insurance company to fill in the blanks in the corporate structure of what was now a growing conglomerate. The Life Insurance Company would be a subsidiary of American Financial, which would then have interests in the financial services of securities, insurance, and real estate. Fred touched base with the advisory committee again. He brought them up to date and discussed his goals. They liked the idea and agreed the company should acquire a life insurance company.

Fred credited the national advertising campaign that Marco Flynn had put together as a primary factor in calming stockholders, quieting the news media, and recruiting new agents. The advertising gained momentum as the national media made it clear that the Equity Funding fraud was unique—a once-in-a-lifetime scam.

American Financial stock resumed its growth. The Company's quarterly 10-K financial report touted financial position and increasing revenues. That gave another boost to the stock price, which passed through fifty dollars a share. The winds were on the stern, and the current was taking American Financial forward.

We're on our way! Fred thought.

***

On Monday, Fred and Jim met with Marco at the Wood Island office.

"Marco, we want to find a life insurance company to issue some policies for us, and reinsure them with Pioneer Life," Fred started. "Bob Green and Eric Steinberg get a lot of life insurance production. They plan to recruit here and back in the Midwest, where they have a lot of connections. Thanks to your efforts with the media over the last few months, Marco, the money we've used for magazine advertising has been well spent."

"I'm not surprised," Marco said. "I knew it wouldn't be long before you would search for your own life insurance company." He told Fred he would stay in California a while longer and look for a potential life insurance company in Northern California, but he was aching to get back to Susan and the children. Marco decided his plan to move back to Florida and rejoin his wife and family needed to be put on the back burner until he completed the assigned task.

Marco visited two small life insurance companies in California. One was at San Bernardino in Southern California, and the other was near Davis, about 45 miles north of the company's home office in Greenbrae. David Walsh & Company assisted Marco in his search. Jones & Peterson, the company's underwriter, also gave him some direction. He reviewed a life insurance company in Palo Alto, American Pacific Life Insurance Company. The search finally narrowed down to two companies—the one in Davis and American Pacific Life in Palo Alto.

Fred didn't think the one in Davis would be a smooth fit. Its location was in the middle of a shopping center, and the management quibbled whether it should be acquired. Marco removed that company from his list.

American Pacific Life, located northwest of San Jose near Stanford, had sufficient technical support available in Santa Clara County for Fred's expansion plans—and lots of technical talent in the nearby Silicon Valley. The sole owner of American Pacific Life had died without a will or a trust, so the probate court would have to handle distributing the ownership of the company.

Negotiations took the better part of two months. When the court signed off on the sale agreement, which gave the heirs about half cash and the rest in stock, one heir objected to the stock. Marco agreed, and the court ruled American Financial would pay that heir's share in cash.

Fred introduced the new company to his employees at Wood Island and highlighted the benefits of American Financial Planning Corporation owning American Pacific Life Insurance Company. He would need help from Bob Green to do the job right.

Fred told Bud Johnson and his accounting people, "The present management of American Pacific Life has resigned and turned the business and control over to us. We now own American Pacific Life Insurance Company. Bob Green will be the president, and Bud Johnson will take over as Chief Financial Officer. Jim, Rick, and I will be on the board, along with Frank Gavin and Keith Raab. Bob will be moving to Palo Alto, and Eric will manage nationwide insurance production of all life insurance sales from right here at Wood Island. Everyone settled in to prepare for business, growing the new life insurance subsidiary.

***

Marco concluded that the company was on a sound footing. His temporary duty with the advertising campaign and the purchase of American Pacific Life had been completed. He made plans for his return to Susan, and his rapidly maturing family in Pensacola.

Jim, with a frustrated look on his face, approached Marco. "I've got a meeting with Jerry Walsh, a potential new branch manager in Coeur d'Alene, Idaho, the day after tomorrow at the Blackwell Hotel. But I'm on my way to Bakersfield. I can't make both meetings. Coeur d'Alene is a beautiful spot. Have you been there?"

"No, but it's on my bucket list. I'm not sure if it's more of a resort town or a retirement town. But you're right; it's a beautiful place tucked away in the Idaho Mountains. And, I know a Southwest Airlines stewardess who lives there."

"Will you take that meeting for me?" Jim asked. "I've already briefed Jerry Walsh on what our needs are in Idaho. He has met Fred, and I want him to get acquainted with more of our team. But I can't make both meetings. If you can make the trip, you're next."

Jim was not aware that Marco was making plans to get out of his apartment and head back to Florida.

"Sure," Marco said. "I can fly up there tomorrow, grab a motel room, and meet Jerry the next morning. A direct flight will save me some time. I'll fly the Aztec to Pappy Boyington Field at

Hayden, Idaho. I can visit with Jerry Walsh the day after tomorrow and be back here that evening."

***

As Marco neared the Coeur d'Alene Regional Airport in the Aztec, the control tower reported instrument conditions with low ceilings. Marco decided to stay on his visual flight plan and approach the field from the southwest under the clouds. The low clouds forced him to descend. Closer to the ground than he wanted to be, he navigated around the surrounding hilltops. Fifteen minutes. Thirty. The lake and the mountain were north of the airport. He was headed for the field. Low clouds brushed the tops of some hills and obscured his visibility.

Jesus, Marco thought. He dropped lower, turning back and forth among the rolling hilltops. He saw a highway that, according to his charts, would lead him the last few miles to the airport.

Sweat formed on his brow. Fear hit him like ice water. *Can I avoid the rest of the hilltops? I'll take a heading of 050 degrees. Climb. The hell with the highway. They'll spot me when I get high enough.*

He called the tower again. "I need an Air Surveillance Radar (ASR) approach to the airport."

With a strained voice, the tower operator returned Marco's call.

"Recommend a Ground Controlled Approach," the tower operator said with a strained voice. "Besides the low ceiling, there's scud over the field."

At a low altitude, Marco turned right. Then left. He dropped one wing then the other as he zig-zagged his way through the small valleys between the ridges.

"Roger," Marco replied. "I'm switching frequencies for a GCA for runway five."

A United Airlines passenger jet approaching duty runway five prepared for its Ground Controlled Approach to a landing. The GCA radar showed the United aircraft a mile and a half out on its descending glide slope and five hundred feet above the ground as it headed for runway five.

The strong gusty winds blew Marco's Aztec too far from its desired course. Surrounded by hilltops, his plane flew a hundred feet above the ground.

"God damn it!" he muttered. His hands trembled. His teeth clenched. His gut filled with dread.

Marco pulled the plane's nose up from about seventy-five feet over the ground to avoid a hill.

"We've got you on ASR now," the tower reported. "But we can't get you onto a GCA glide path until we get the United flight above you out of your way. Stand by.

"Climb to fifteen hundred feet on your current heading of 050 and execute the missed-approach procedure." The ground controller told the United pilot.

"Roger," the pilot replied and started his climb.

The tower hadn't cleared Marco to climb into the clouds and he zig-zagged through the valleys and around the hilltops. Marco struggled to maintain control of the Aztec. His thoughts

whirled—*what about Susan? What about the kids?*
He tried to calm himself and rely on his training.
But steering around the hills became too difficult.

*Oh, my God. Please, God. For my children's
sake.*

He barreled toward a hilltop—the
surrounding sound a roar. Marco couldn't think.
Attempting to lift the nose, he pulled the Aztec up.
This time harder.

Shit! Susan, I love you.

***

According to the accident report, marks on the
ground indicated that both propellers grazed the
hilltop before the plane crashed into another hill.
Fred refused to believe the news. "Marco is one of
the best instrument pilots I have ever flown with.
There has to be more to the story." He put a
complete investigation into play with the FAA. The
investigation concluded pilot error caused the
accident. The pilot should have been on an
instrument flight plan, not a visual flight plan.

Except for essential tasks, the company
closed on Friday and remain closed over the

weekend. Fred asked employees to observe a moment of silence. "Marco had a great love for the company," Fred said, "and had given it his dedicated service."

It was unfortunate, astounding, that Marco had no significant life insurance, had not made a current financial plan, and had left everything to Susan in his trust. He wanted to make sure she was financially comfortable. The trust left Susan with Marco's American Financial stock, a small accidental death life insurance policy, his ten-thousand-dollar life insurance policy from the Marine Corps, and the house with no mortgage.

The loss of Marco Flynn devastated Fred. Memories flooded him. He and Marco had enjoyed flying their jet fighter planes around New Orleans on reserve duty weekends. He recalled those times when the two of them would take off from New Orleans Naval Air Station in their A-4s, climb out from the field to join up, and then head for Kansas City or Indianapolis or Dallas to enjoy the rest of the weekend before taking both birds back home. They often shared sea stories in one of their cars driving back and forth between Pensacola and New Orleans on a duty weekend. He could not forget those wonderful annual reunions with their Marine Corps buddies at Cherry Point North Carolina; it was so much fun sharing time with other friends they had flown with in the Marine Corps in the past. While he was in Pensacola for the funeral, Fred immersed himself in long spells of silence.

When he returned to Wood Island, he thrust his way into creating a conglomerate. Financial planning, the immediate task ahead, sat foremost in his mind.

CHAPTER ELEVEN

Proxy Fight

The economic recovery from the recession was a 'U-Shaped Recovery,' a type of economic recovery that experiences a gradual decline followed by a gradual rise back to its previous peak. Fred had waited the better part of a decade, and he was ready for the recovery to get legs. The major influence of this recession was stagflation in the country— inflation climbed, even as unemployment rose. Other factors included massive government spending on the Vietnam War and the Wall Street stock market crash in mid-decade.

Fred counted on better times ahead. The nation became a society afflicted by a deep cultural malaise. In 1974, President Nixon accepted high inflation but not high unemployment. He convinced the Federal Reserve Board to assist him with his political objectives of cheap money and low-interest rates. This would promote growth in the short-term, which helped American Financial. Its common stock passed fifty-three dollars a share. But it was not a recipe for economic growth.

***

A reassessment of the human assets of American Financial became imperative. Integrating Cohen & Company increased real estate activity. Marty viewed business from the perspective of Cohen & Company. One of his officers in Long Beach was developing time shares. He was comfortable with the plans moving forward, and knew he could operate his firm within the umbrella of American Financial. He still longed for a connection with the Wall Street brokerage firm that United Express owned, and his hope for getting in to REITS had not subsided.

Losing Marco Flynn and restarting a new life insurance company required Fred to view things differently. Jim was a great recruiter, and was satisfied to strengthen those talents in California and Oregon. American Pacific Life Insurance

Company increased life and annuity sales with Bob and Eric in the rest of the country. Rick Taylor was comfortable practicing law with Woodford and Hoskins, finally realizing the fruits of his dream.

With Fred's leadership, the company was on the move again. By 1976, American Financial was a significant player in the Financial Services Industry. The company emphasized a team approach to management with an eye to windward for the consumer. Now a public corporation, the 10 Q quarterly report to the Securities and Exchange Commission was due.

Fred and Bud went over the draft. Bud delivered the report to Ron at David Walsh & Company for a review by the certified public accountant before filing. In a competitive environment of short-term growth, Fred Maloney was elated that his company was doing so well.

While returning his copy of the draft of Form 10 Q report to his file drawer, Fred received a phone call from Cat Cay in the Bahamas.

"Hello, Fred. How have you been?" Fred recognized the sing-song lilt of Charles De Long's voice. "I'm sorry to hear about Marco Flynn. He was a good man."

"Thank you, Mr. De Long. We miss Marco."

"I know we haven't kept in touch since you rejected my offer to buy your corporate bonds, and we parted in Cincinnati. I've been tied up with Lincoln Savings and Loan."

"I wouldn't say we parted in Cincinnati, since you never showed," Fred jabbed.

"You have done very well with American Financial in this economy." Charles Keating ignored Fred's comment. "That Equity Funding disaster didn't slow you down for long. I'll be in San Francisco in the next couple of days. Let's get together."

"I understand from the news reports you have taken another step into the S&L business, and you're getting some help from the United States Congress."

"We're doing well—those Washington rumors are groundless—we're doing it on our own, thank you. Middle America still needs help with their savings. I've watched your company since you were last in Cincinnati. Your recent financial reports look good. I can't wait to see your current 10 Q report. You have done an excellent job serving the middle class in America. I like that. They need homes.

"Banks focus on how to loan money to businesses rather than lending to individuals for home ownership. The interest rates are elevated, and inflation even higher. I've never seen anything like it. The savings and loan industry is poised for a ride when the economy recovers, and that's for damn sure. Let's get together and talk."

"What do you want to talk about, Charles?"

"Well, there's a lot to talk about. I see some compatibility in serving our respective customers. Clients need access to the financial products that your company offers. I know it's not just life insurance and mutual funds—like it was when you came to Cincinnati to get money."

Fred heard him draw on a cigarette

"People are talking about financial planning," De Long continued. "If it gets legs, it could be a new industry raising its head."

That got Fred's attention.

"Where would we do that?" Fred asked sarcastically. "The last time you and I planned to meet, I was at your office in Cincinnati, and you were on your boat in the Florida Keys or the Bahamas."

"This time, I'll meet you in San Francisco. And no boat. I'll be there next week. Can we get together?"

"Probably. I could meet you in the City, or you can catch the ferry from Fisherman's Wharf to Larkspur, and I can pick you up there. It's near my office. Let me know what you prefer, and we can set a time."

That son of a bitch. I don't know why I am wasting a good day on him. But you never know. No personal guarantees. He must be thinking he can bet on us now. I wonder what he wants. We've come too far not to check it out. I guess I've got nothing to lose but a trip to The City.

***

Fred drove across the bridge to the Commonwealth Club at the foot of Market Street. The Club provided a comfortable environment for business meetings. Fred could have taken the ferry, but he thought he would stop by the San Francisco office on his way back and visit with Phil Schmidt.

When he arrived, Fred found De Long and two of his financial people in the bar. After introductions, Fred took them to the temporary office on the first floor reserved for members.

Following a short discussion of the economy, Mr. De Long laid it on the line. "I want to buy American Financial Planning Corporation. Let me show you how well American Financial will fold into my conglomerate. An all-cash deal—a chance for you to take the profits from all your hard work. I want to keep you, Jim Barns, and Marty Cohen with the company. You and Jim have a lot of control over the stock. Our investment bankers think this could be a win-win situation for both companies.

"I'll be setting aside our quest for saving and loans for the time being while we resolve some regulatory issues. I think, with the reach we already have in the Midwest, your company would be a natural fit for us. Especially with the life insurance operation you've got going back there.

"As you know, we've wanted to get into the life insurance business and offer additional products to the S&Ls we already own. American Financial would give us an additional product fit."

"Slow down, Charles," Fred said. "I'm *not* interested in being part of a conglomerate—yours or any other. We prefer to tend to our own business. We've worked too long and hard to become a financial company, and we're well on our way. Getting sidetracked by a merger with you or anyone else is not in our business plan."

He's a confident guy, Fred thought. *I like that. And he's a gambler; I'll give him that. He's taking a long shot. It's all I can do to keep from laughing.*

Charles persisted. "Midwest Financial has an advantage you don't have—cash. Your expertise and our money would serve your long-range plan to introduce financial planning to the middle class. That was your goal when we first talked in Cincinnati. I presume it still is. It's a perfect fit with my saving and loan customers."

"You're right about that. Our seminars and our growing sales force have us well positioned for that."

After the better part of an hour, Mr. De Long summarized. "Look Fred, I know how you feel about staying independent. But I want to buy American Financial—all cash. I'm prepared to file proxy material with the SEC and the State of California to get it. I'll offer your shareholders eight percent over the current market price of their American Financial stock. If a majority of your shareholders vote to sell, Midwest Financial will buy all of the American Financial stock. In today's environment, it should be very tempting to your shareholders. With your support, this could be easily accomplished. We could work together to get the information needed for the proxy material."

This guy is out to lunch! I can't believe he's serious. No contact since I was in Cincinnati, and he wasn't even there. He sounds sincere, but I'll be damned if he'll take me to the cleaners twice. I don't care how much money he has; I am not interested.

"Charles, you can take your money back to Cincinnati. American Financial is not for sale. And I've got to go. It's time for my next meeting. I don't want to get stuck in the evening commute."

"If you don't help with a friendly tender offer, I'll file for an adverse proxy vote to get the American Financial stock," Charles said. "I think it'll be difficult for your public shareholders to agree with your feelings about independence. Many of them need cash these days. I didn't think you'd favor a friendly tender offer. If you don't, fine. I'm prepared to make an adverse tender offer. If we have to go adverse to get the company, we'll increase our offer, probably to ten percent above market price instead of eight."

Insulted, Fred smashed out his Marlboro in the glass ashtray and looked De Long directly in the eye. "Go ahead and file your damn adverse proxy material, Charles. We're not going to help you upset our company. Our shareholders are loyal. You won't get a positive vote from them."

Fred got up and left. He didn't bother to say goodbye.

***

Fred located a telephone in the Commonwealth Club and filled Peggy in on the meeting.

Flabbergasted, Peggy said, "I can't believe that you would get up and walk out after getting such a proposal. What if he's able to do it?"

"Honey, I'm not going to play his game. I almost did before, and it nearly ruined me. We're doing fine on our own. Besides, I don't want to get mixed up with him anyway."

"Are you sure? You could have at least gotten more information before you said no."

"I'll tell you more about it when I get home. I love you."

***

That evening, Fred and Peggy sat by the guest house near the pool. Fred lit a Marlboro while

Peggy poured coffee. "Where's this coming from? Why does Mr. De Long want to buy us now? Isn't this the same man who ignored you when you went back to Cincinnati? What are we going to do?"

"I told him no and that I'd fight when he files a proxy fight . . . *if* he files for one."

"How do you think the shareholders will vote if he files? A lot of them have some outstanding profits built up in their stock."

"I know. My job is to do the best I can for my stockholders. I don't think De Long will be able to help me with that task. If he does file for a proxy, every share will count. With Marco's death, Susan Flynn is our largest shareholder."

"Really?" Peggy never thought about that. *Marco is dead, and Sue is alone.*

"Marco kept buying our private stock before we went public. Susan's vote is important. Would you call her in Pensacola and tell her about what's going on? Ask her to vote 'no' to the acquisition if there is a proxy. I'll be happy to talk with her by phone if she has any questions you can't answer."

"I'll be glad to. Sue and I talk often."

***

Peggy called Susan and explained the situation.

"I wasn't expecting anybody to try to buy our stock," Susan said. "I'm happy to do whatever I can for you, Fred, and the company. Marco said to hold on to the company stock if anything ever happened to him," Susan said.

"If Mr. De Long goes ahead with his threat to file legal papers, you may receive proxy materials in the mail. Fred told him the company is not for sale. A ballot allows you to record your vote. The proxy gives you a choice to vote for the offer and sell your stock or vote against it and keep it. You check the 'no' box and mail it in."

"Yes, of course," Susan said.

Peggy called Fred. "Don't worry about Susan. She'll do whatever she can to help us. If she gets a proxy, she will vote against the sale to Midwest Financial and mail it right back."

***

When Susan received the proxy materials, she marked the 'no' box and put the proxy form in the mail. On that weekend, John Danford came to

Susan's house to discuss the new American Financial sale. Susan didn't tell her father she'd already voted not to sell, signed the proxy, and had mailed it in.

Mr. Danford had already reviewed his proxy material. "I think you should take advantage of the generous cash offer, Susan—eight percent over the current market price of your stock. You should cast your vote to sell. It's the best move for the financial security of your family. It's a generous cash offer. Vote to sell."

"But Dad, Marco told me if anything happened to him, I should hold on to the shares of American Financial stock."

"Susan, Marco didn't know that the economy would get worse. Cash gets eaten up by inflation. If inflation keeps rising, your dollars won't pay for your daily needs. Take the cash and put it into long-term certificates of deposit while interest rates are so high."

Susan felt a twinge of remorse. What would she tell Peggy? She wanted to help the Maloneys, but her father made a good point. She got up from the couch, went upstairs, and checked the children. After, she stepped into her room, let the tears spill from her eyes, wiped her face, and returned downstairs.

"Are you sure you're not still angry because Marco didn't take up your offer to join your firm after he graduated from Stanford?"

"No, darling. It's not that. Selling your stock with that generous percentage increase in the stock price is the best move for you and the children."

"You're right. I know I should follow your advice. But I already voted 'no' and mailed the proxy in." She tried to wipe the tears from her eyes.

"*What*!"

Susan wished she could sink into the couch and disappear. Marco's advice to Susan had been clear. She was afraid of the anger on her father's face. He was right. She had to take care of her family. After some agonizing thought, she decided to change her vote. "Okay Dad, I'll change my vote to 'yes'. But how do I do that?

Susan's father took a deep breath, and sighed. "Well Susan, you'll have to sign another proxy and vote 'yes'. I have a few shares of the stock myself, but I didn't send my proxy in. I thought my shares were too few to make a difference. You can use my proxy form, Sign it right here." He laid the paper on the table in front of her. "We'll have to move quickly. The vote is the day after tomorrow. It's already too late to mail it."

"What are we going to do?" Susan said bewildered.

"One of us will have to carry it back. The mail won't get there in time."

"Dad, I can't possibly go on such short notice. Why don't we just let it go?"

"You have a huge block of stock, Susan. I checked with my broker yesterday, and he told me it looks like the vote will be close. If you sign the substitute proxy, I'll take it back. Selling the company is in your best interest. It's the least I can do for you and my grandchildren. I'll call my travel agent and schedule a flight to San Francisco."

***

Jim met Marty in the conference room at Wood Island. Papers were spread all over the conference table. They were discussing one of Marty's new limited partnerships when Fred came in and pulled up a chair on the other side of the table. Fred had just returned from his appointment with Charles De Long in San Francisco, and his head still spun. Marty gathered his papers, and placed them into his brief case. They considered the ramifications they now faced. Fred's jaw tightened, and his brow furrowed as he saw their muted reaction to his meeting with De Long.

"I'm confident Susan Flynn's vote will carry the day by rejecting the initial offer Charles De Long plans to make for the company. "Guys," Fred said as he glanced at the two men. "Charles De Long is serious. He wants to buy American Financial Planning Corporation. He says he'll offer eight percent above the current market price of our stock to our shareholders, but only if we support his proxy bid. If we don't support his eight percent bid, he'll file a second proxy—an adverse one—and raise his bid to ten percent over the market price, all cash.

"He plans to present his first offer to our shareholders right away, and wants our support. He thinks the stockholders will jump at the eight percent offer—-a substantial offer in the current economy, and he won't have to file a second proxy offer . . . if we help him with the first offer."

Jim had not been in favor of Fred talking with Charles De Long. After the debacle in Cincinnati, he did not want Fred to, once again, waste time dealing with De Long.

Tired of the daily struggle and frustrated, Jim was comfortable with the way the company operated now. He was against a merger, but he did think about getting some cash out of all the American Financial stock he held.

Charles De Long was a strong advocate, but Fred had made up his mind. He refused to let the company be bought for the eight percent bid. He didn't believe De Long would file a second offer if he lost the first vote. The public shareholders, however, might see it differently because of the horrid economy.

Jim supported Fred's objection to the first proxy but wanted to support the larger, ten percent bid if the first bid failed. In his mind, Jim was already spending the cash. He told Fred he would vote no on the first offer of eight percent and encourage his sales force to do the same. He was silent on the possibility of a second vote.

***

Marty decided that he could have it both ways: if the corporation was sold, he could take his own company out of the mix, go back to Long Beach, and keep selling limited partnerships with a new boss. If it didn't get sold, Marty wanted to maintain a good rapport with Fred, going forward. He vote 'no', and then wait and see. Marty's mental wheels turned as he watched Fred light a Marlboro. *My best shot is to help defeat the first vote. When it comes to a second proxy vote, I will have plenty of negotiating room to deal with whatever is available at that time.*

Marty knew that he could leave his company and take the cash if either proxy offer was accepted, and then be free to rebuild Cohen & Company in

Southern California on his own terms. When he joined the company several years before, he only had agreed to stay on if the company remained independent. If the company sold, he could leave and take his company with him. He decided to vote 'no', and the wait and see what De Long was going to do.

Marty looked directly at Fred. "Mr. De Long is a poor negotiator. I'm with you on rejecting his first offer. We need to inform our friends and shareholders to do the same. Then, if Mr. De Long is as hungry as he appears to be, he'll file another proxy. That's when we can decide whether to switch and jump on his bandwagon. That would give him what he needs to help him sell his second tender offer to the shareholders, and in this economy, it could be the way to go."

Fred was disappointed. He paced around the room. He saw that neither Jim nor Marty wanted to go any further with the conversation. "They'll both vote against the proxy." He turned to go back to his office, with heavy heart.

Jim Barns showed no emotion. He looked uncomfortable in his chair and twirled his ballpoint pen between his fingers. He told Marty "I'll support Fred on fighting the eight percent offer, but I think De Long might win that vote. Let's wait and see. Our shareholders have a lot of profit in their American Financial stock. In these days, I think they'll take the money and run. We'll see what happens."

Following the meeting with Fred, Jim considered the cash he would have if De Long's offer went to a second vote. He wasn't comfortable telling Fred he'd support a "no" vote on the second proxy. Fortunately, Fred didn't ask him. Jim hadn't given any thought to Susan Flynn's shares. *If there's a second vote, I'll vote yes and take the cash. I like Marty's suggestion to help Fred kill the first proxy with the hope that Charles De Long files a second proxy and makes a higher offer. I have no desire to work with the worm after he demanded personal guarantees at the last minute when Fred was in Cincinnati. Marty's suggestion makes sense. I'll wait and see how it goes.*

Back in his office, Fred realized that Jim was not as enthusiastic about financial planning as Fred thought he was. It hadn't occurred him that Jim could even hesitate to vote "no" on the first proxy. He knew that Jim didn't want to work for Charles De Long and that he would pitch in to get the shareholders to reject the buy-out offer.

If there was a second proxy vote, Marty realized he might have some support from Jim. He would still stand with Fred on the first ballot. He called several salesmen in Southern California and told them, in confidence, about the possibility of a second vote. Marty asked them to reject the initial eight percent offer and to pass the word along to other limited-partnership salesmen.

"Management has enough votes to reject the first offer, but the second, higher offer from Midwest Financial could look good if the first one fails," Marty told his salesmen. "Vote 'no'. If there's a second vote, vote 'yes,' and take your profits. If the second vote is to sell, keep working with me at Cohen & Company.

***

Fred called Bill Bretton in New York to confirm that United Express would vote their American Financial shares against being acquired by Midwest Financial.

"I think United Express will vote its stock against the acquisition," Bill told Fred. "We like the way you're running American Financial. We want you to stay independent. Between you and me, I don't trust Charles De Long."

Fred did not like the tone of Bill's response. Bill had said the right words, but Fred sensed reluctance. Fred felt a merger with American Financial had always been on Bill's mind—after all, that was his job at United Express.

Fred then called the company's underwriters, Jones & Peterson, and asked how they thought the shareholders would vote.

***

On Friday, before the scheduled vote, Fred and Rick ate lunch at the restaurant in the Wells Fargo building. That building—another structure built in the 1800s—was made when they dredged the Bay shoreline.

"The votes will be counted by noon on Monday, Rick. I doubt there will even be a second proxy offer from Charles De Long." He told Rick about Susan's decision to vote against the proxy. "Cliff Kunkel, at Jones & Peterson, said his people have learned the SEC is considering initiating charges against Charles De Long early next year. They have honed in on reports that a senator from Ohio and a congressman from Arizona unlawfully supported Mr. De Long's plan to petition for some rule changes for the savings and loan industry.

"That could be a major trouble for the CEO of a listed company," Rick replied.

"He also told me that an Ohio newspaper is investigating claims by a local savings and loan that Midwest Financial Corporation had defrauded the newspaper. There are no regulatory findings yet. The SEC has filed no charges against Midwest Financial or against Charles De Long at this time."

***

On Monday, Jones & Peterson finished the official counting at noon. The vote to reject the offer from

Midwest Financial won by just under one percent of the votes cast.

One percent? He threw his ballpoint pen towards the wastebasket in the corner of his office. Bulls-eye—right in the bucket. *I thought we would win, but didn't know it would be this close. We have to buckle down and be what we are—a conglomerate, not a stockbroker. Our stockholders realize we're the leading financial company focused on what America needs most in this weak economy—mutual funds, life insurance, and limited partnerships for small businesses.*

***

When Susan's father arrived at the polling location, the counting of the ballots was already completed, and Cliff Kunkle had certified the results. Fred returned to his office to put out the word. Several clerks stood nearby, organizing papers when Mr. Danford arrived. He approached Cliff Kunkle, muttering something about "the damn traffic" and "lots of taxi cabs."

The proxy board showed the result—reject Midwest Financial's offer to buy the stock of

American Financial Planning Corporation. The vote count by Jones & Petersen was 50.3% to reject the Midwest Financial offer, 49.7% to accept it. The Company would not be sold to Midwest Financial. This vote count included Susan's original proxy vote to reject the offer.

Mr. Danford thrust Susan's second proxy vote accepting the Midwest Financial offer into Cliff Kunkel's hands. Cliff turned to one of his assistants and discussed the late vote.

"Let's get on with it," Mr. Danford growled.

"I'm sorry, Mr. Danford," Cliff Kunkel said. "The official vote has been taken and counted. The vote count rejects the proxy offer of Midwest Financial to buy American Financial."

"I demand a recount."

"There will be no recount. The revised vote of Mrs. Flynn is not included in the vote count."

"On behalf of my daughter, I demand a recount. I'm her attorney."

"I don't think there will be a recount. You could ask management for another vote if you wish.

We counted the ballots, and the vote will stand as counted.

"I demand a recount." Mr. Danford thrust Susan's revised proxy at Cliff Knuckle once again.

"The time for voting has passed," he told Mr. Danford. "The shares originally voted by Mrs. Flynn were received within the time allotted. Her subsequent submission was not. Jones & Petersen has certified that American Financial will remain private based on legal voting within the prescribed time. The revised proxy vote of Mrs. Flynn is rejected."

Outraged, Charles De Long joined the discussion. "The first vote was not complete," he told Chris Kunkel. "Mrs. Flynn can change her vote. She signed a subsequent official ballot. There is no controversy about that! The substitute proxy, duly executed by Mrs. Flynn, must be counted."

John Danford approached Cliff Kunkle again and pushed Mr. De Long aside. "I am an attorney, Mr. Kunkel, and I know proxy rules. The change of a vote at this point is within the proxy rules of the State of California. I will direct her attorneys here in San Francisco to file a lawsuit in the California court to apply for a restraining order to prevent Jones & Petersen from rejecting the changed vote of Susan Flynn."

"Go ahead and file your lawsuit, Mr. Danford. The vote stands as counted. The stockholders reject the Midwest Financial offer."

With that, Mr. Danford stomped out of the room. Mr. De Long followed.

In his hotel room, Charles De Long considered his options. *The change of vote should have been allowed. Given the time it took for him to travel from Pensacola to the ballot counting, Mr. Danford did all he could. With Mrs. Flynn's new vote, we would own American Financial. A recount gives us a victory. My lawyer will get this vote turned around.*

***

Fred held a victory party in the conference room at the Wood Island office on Wednesday. A great variety of food and drink packed the long conference table. Jubilance filled the room. Many of the local business people in the Greenbrae area joined employees, their spouses, and friends.

Fred took the microphone. "Marty Cohen's people put an incredible amount of energy into the fight," Fred announced as he stood before the crowd. "Jim, Bob, and Eric did a great job getting their sales forces, who held company stock, to vote to defeat Midwest Financial's proxy. "A toast to all who voted to reject the Midwest Financial offer."

Everyone lifted glasses. A cheer went up from those gathered around the conference table.

"And here's to our new course with American Pacific Life, and the work that our new people have done," Jim added.

"And finally, a toast to the future of American Financial Planning Corporation—-and to the company's stockholders."

Fred did not realize how much Jim Barns had hoped for a "yes" vote, and how much he hoped for a second proxy vote.

***

The California court rejected the petition filed by John Danford and Charles De Long for a restraining order. The court allowed the vote rejecting the acquisition of American Financial by Midwest Financial to stand. When Charles De Long heard the news, he threw a book across the room. "Shit!"

Charles De Long knew his board of directors had not yet approved the second proxy offer of ten percent over the price of American Financial stock if the first offer of eight percent failed. He was confident of his ability to convince the board to take the next step. They had supported all of his ventures with the savings and loan industry, but he did worry about the federal and state investigations into his activities.

***

It was Saturday morning, and the office was closed. Fred made some coffee, lit a Marlboro, and plunked down in the leather swivel chair at his desk. *Well,* he thought. *We've got our ship sailing again. I don't think there will be a second proxy. Jones & Peterson highlighted some of the legal issues they could be facing, and a new ten percent proxy will be expensive for them. It's time to concentrate on building this company up. Jim is focused on adding to his sales force, but his concerns about catching up with Bob and Eric have him a little offtrack. Moving ahead with financial planning isn't even on his radar while I've achieved another item on my bucket list—running a conglomerate.*

Bill Bretton's tone of voice still concerned Fred when Bill told him United Express would back him in the proxy fight and vote the shares of our stock they own against the acquisition.

He called Bill from the office and relayed the good news of the court action. "I doubt there will be another offer, Bill. Thanks for the support from United Express." Unable to hide his elation, Fred's voice cracked with emotion. "It's been a long haul, Bill, but Equity Funding is in the background now. The company is on solid financial footing and set on building a conglomerate that will carve a new path, including financial planning for Mid America.

"Good, Fred. Congratulations. This news will thrill Howard Roberts. He wants to know if you can fill us in on the details the next time you are in

New York. We're looking forward to working with you."

On Monday, Fred asked his secretary to schedule a flight to New York. Still exhausted from the tense battle he had endured, Fred could only thank God for the gift of allowing the first proxy vote by Susan Flynn to stand. He often thought how close he had come to losing his company into the confusion of the savings and loan industry. The fact that Charles De Long might drag in a bad reputation from his lobbying efforts with Congress also had concerned Fred.

Fred kept asking himself why he'd decided to fly to New York. He had often thought about doing joint seminars with United Express around the country. If the two companies could get along without fighting with each other over common products, it could work well. But that was a big 'if'. A small vacation with Peggy might have been better medicine than this trip to New York.

The United Express driver picked up Fred's bag, put it in the back of the limo, and took him through the afternoon traffic to the World Trade

Center. Still unsettled, Fred retrieved a Marlboro from his shirt pocket and pushed the lighter button near the backseat door handle. He wanted to be on an even keel when he met with Howard Roberts.

Nervous, but not sure why, Fred had felt an overture in Bill's voice on that phone call when Bill mentioned working closer together. But something behind the comment that unsettled Fred. *If United Express is thinking about a merger with us, I will shut that off at the pass. I have to get to New York and find out where United Express stands.*

The more he thought about it, the more Fred hoped he'd misread Bill's comment. He knew of Howard Roberts' interest in the financial seminars American Financial used to attract new customers, but wasn't sure how far United Express wanted to go. Fred had made it clear he intended to keep control of the American Financial Planning Corporation. He had his own ship to sail.

Certificates and photographs of Bill Bretton with powerful men filled the walls in his office. Fred selected a comfortable leather chair and pulled it closer to the ashtray. He lit another Marlboro, exhaled the smoke, and took a sip of coffee. From the top of the World Trade Center, the world looked bright.

"Howard Roberts has studied the offer that Midwest Financial put on the table with their proxy and your firm's response to your shareholders. You deserve congratulations on the victory. My people tell me that the proxy fight by Midwest Financial is probably over, and you will remain independent. We don't believe that Midwest Financial will come up with the ten percent offer Mr. De Long planned to make. Howard thinks he sees a natural affinity between United Express and American Financial."

Wow! *I've thought a lot about the compatibility of the United Express Company with my vision of financial planning over the years, but I never saw it as a realistic goal. They're just too big. Their structure, and the use of their Wall Street broker, Levy Loeb Rhodes, to market Marty's real estate products, would have been perfect. It could have been ideal. But now, we can handle a new course on our own and still work with Levy Loeb Rhodes on their real estate investment trusts*

(REITs). *Marty Cohen is excited with the possibility of creating some of his own REITs.*

"I've spoken with Howard about an acquiring your firm on several occasions," Bill continued, "before Midwest Financial came into the picture. As head of mergers and acquisitions, I later told him I wished we had thought of you as an acquisition before Midwest Financial came along. I always felt your company could be a good fit for us."

"I've worked long and hard to steer this company toward financial planning," Fred said. "And, I don't want to be somebody else's employee."

"I understand that, Fred. But my M & A people report that the odds of you staying independent for the long haul are slim. You're getting too big to be a one-man show."

"Bill, you know that I've discarded my goal of being the second funding company in the United States when the Equity Funding scandal got legs. But I do believe that America Financial can lead with financial planning for the middle class in the next few years, even without funding. Financial planning is coming; count on it. I don't think it would be healthy for us to get wrapped into another company, even yours. Not at this point."

"Hold it," Bill replied. "You're known for your patience, Fred. Howard thinks like you do and knows you won't fit into a box. He likes your premise about the financial services industry and is encouraged by your long view. We have people working on new investment vehicles all the time— no-load mutual funds, for example."

"I'm glad to hear that; those funds will be good for the middle class," Fred said. "But I'm not sure our key people would hang around as employees of a larger company. If there were a merger, Jim Barns might come under Howard Roberts at your United American Life Insurance Company anyway, and he wouldn't like that. Jim calls his own shots. I can see Bob and Eric staying around at American Pacific Life, at least until United Express decides how to operate with two different life insurance subsidiaries on two different coasts. After that, I don't know."

"Those points are well taken," Bill said. "Let's go downstairs."

***

Howard Roberts greeted Fred with a smile, offered his hand, and invited both men to his leather sofa. Howard's office exhibited the tributes of power. In his early sixties, he'd come a long way since taking over United Express. His hair was only now turning gray where its edges neared his ears. He stood straight and moved about with ease in his Brooks Brothers suit. It was obvious how comfortable Howard was at the helm of the world's largest payments company.

"Thanks for stopping by to see us, Fred. I think this is an important moment."

"Thanks, Howard, it's always nice to see you. Bill filled me in on your views of the future of seminars and financial planning. I want to hear more."

After a lengthy discussion about the direction of financial planning and the use of seminars, Howard threw a curveball.

"I understand what you must be thinking—I wouldn't give up my position as chief executive officer any more than you would. United Express needs your talent and ambition at the highest level if we want to make inroads into actual financial planning.

"We've discussed that point at our board meetings. I'm confident the board will endorse my position that your leadership will be needed if we are to reach that goal together. I think we're both talking in terms of years, not months."

"You are certainly right about the time frame." Fred glanced out the window. *Where's he going with this?* Fred wondered. *Howard talks as if he owns American Financial. He must have something in mind since he hasn't let the subject drop. I made it clear I'd be sailing my own ship. A company can't have two Chief Executive Officers.*

"This is my thought, Fred, *not* a promise. If United Express wants to make a substantial footprint in financial planning with its credit card and brokerage facilities, you should be at the helm." Howard looked directly at Fred; they were eye to eye. "You know where the rocks and shoals are, and we'll provide the necessary resources. I want to recommend that United Express Company sets up a permanent ad hoc committee to develop a financial planning capability. You'll be the chairman. You would continue to run American Financial—that's the most certain way we can get from here to there. Again Fred, not a promise—an idea."

"It's a fascinating thought," Fred replied. "But you're right. I'm not giving up the CEO position of my company. Things move like molasses in a large corporation, even yours, Howard. Altering our strategic plan would water down the synergies we have developed at American Financial."

"I hear you," Howard replied.

"Following your line of thinking," Fred doodled on a corner of his notepad. "Let me give you and Bill a different scenario. Given the premise that our two companies could work together toward financial planning rather than be competitors, we should consider a joint venture and—"

"Where in the world is that coming from?" Bill interrupted.

Howard cut him off. "Let him talk, Bill."

"Our attorney, Rick Taylor, has done research on the subject. He thinks a joint venture could be set up as a California corporation with its separate charter and objectives. The joint venture would have its management structure and would exist as a separate corporation under California law. United Express and American Financial would be the sole owners of that joint venture. Each company would put up half the initial funding for half of the ownership."

Howard turned to Bill with a smile. "Could be a realistic alternative to an acquisition. Have your people look into it." He glanced at Fred and then back to Bill. "Our lawyers are at your disposal, Bill. Have them consult with Rick Taylor."

The three men shook hands, and Fred returned to San Francisco.

Relaxed, yet almost giddy, Fred took his seat on the plane. A joint venture with United Express excited him. Without being acquired, he could still run American Financial while having a reliable partner at United Express to pursue an area of common objectives.

He hadn't realized that Howard Roberts had ventured so far into the concept of financial planning for customers of both companies. Fred also viewed it as a needed challenge to delivering financial products and services to Middle America—a trusted old company and a dynamic new company working towards a common cause.

**

The United Express Company had always been an innovative company. In the 1950s, they offered personal, business, and corporate credit cards, and introduced the green charge card. They diversified by buying a major casualty insurance company in the 1960s. Later, they acquired a Wall Street stock brokerage firm. Fred thought a joint venture between American Financial and United Express could provide a link between personal travel planning services and personal financial planning services.

Fred took the time to call each member of his advisory committee and asked for their thoughts. The reaction of each member was the same. All agreed that working with a major company like United Express made sense—Fred should pursue building a cohesive connection, "to the bitter end," as Keith Raab said.

Fred thought about Keith's comment as he finished the calls. He took a deep breath. *What a complete turn of events. We've moved from pioneers through the unknown, to the mountain top. There are a few broken arrows on the ground, but no arrows in our chests. From dreams and hard work, a new company will evolve. Our journey will give families affordable life planning and credit cards. Financial planning will finally be accepted, and grow.*

Fred met with Jim, Rick, and Bud Johnson at the Wood Island conference room. They reviewed the substance of Fred's meetings in New York. Fred wanted to have Bud's input as Chief Financial Officer in case they wanted to go over some numbers.

"What do you mean, they thought about acquiring us if the Midwest Financial offer fell through? That's way out in right field—-not even in the ballpark." Jim's jaw dropped. He slammed his pen onto his yellow pad and stood up. Anger curled his lips. "Charles De Long said he was going to follow up with a new vote at a higher price for our stock. We should wait and see what he comes up with. Everyone is working hard to get our stock price up before De Long comes up with the second proxy offer. We'll get even more money for our stock if the price of our stock keeps rising ahead of the next vote. Ten percent, he said. That'll be ten percent of a higher number for the next proxy. We should be focused on our own goals, not some financial planning project that you and Howard Roberts are taken up with. Let's focus on life insurance."

Rick stopped making notes on his pad, tapped his pen on the conference room table, and glanced at the other men. Jim sat down, closed his briefcase, and looked like he planned to leave the room. He squirmed in his chair, obviously uncomfortable with the whole conversation.

Rick continued. "Howard Roberts must have had his lawyers and Bill's people up all night thinking about a joint venture between the corporations. That's a quantum leap. I know you asked me to research the idea, Fred, but I didn't think you would present it to the chief executive officer of United Express so effectively——or so soon."

Bud Johnson joined in. "United Express hasn't even looked at our books and records. There wasn't that much information in the proxy materials already filed by Midwest Financial. United Express has its own life insurance and mutual fund companies. So do we. I can't imagine how they could put all those pieces together for a joint venture so quickly."

"There's no putting together," Fred responded. "Howard Roberts is considering a new idea for his company. His people will be coming here to talk. I told Howard Roberts and Bill Bretton that we are not for sale—they accept that now and are no longer discussing a merger. We can have our cake and eat it too. Howard Roberts likes the concept. We'll have an opportunity to talk about it while Bill and his people are out here."

Rick agreed. "You and Howard Roberts have a common goal: reform some of the practices of the financial services industry by developing new financial products and services and creating practical methods of accumulating and maintaining family wealth for Middle America. You both see financial planning as a stepping stone in that direction. Mr. Roberts has been an innovator ever since started transforming the United Express Company—it won't stop now."

"That's a mouthful," Bud Johnson said. "Read that back to me in plain English."

"Let's start with the possible joint venture that Fred is talking about. Two corporations create a new business entity. That business entity would have shared ownership, shared returns, and shared risk. It would select its chief executive officer. A joint venture could access a new market, for example, financial planning. Fred proposes we join

with United Express to form a new legal entity—
let's call it American United Financial Partners, a
joint venture."

"Howard Roberts doesn't want to purchase
us, and we don't want to sell our company to him,"
Fred added. "However, with a joint venture, we can
put capital, talent, and energy together and get
results. The joint venture can operate under its own
name and have its own liabilities, separate from
each company. Half of the stock will be owned by
each corporation."

Rick added, "Operating as a partnership
would be too slow and too risky for either of us.
This way, we would each own half of the joint
venture. That entity would assume all the risks and
pass on all profits, one-half to each owner."

As Jim digested the conversation, he began
to see the light. He could see where Fred wanted to
go, and he did not like the idea of getting further
away from life insurance. "I've got one of the three
votes on our board of directors. If the joint venture
comes up for a vote, mine is 'no'. I'm pretty much
fed up with this whole financial planning track that

you are on, Fred. I know that financial planning works well, but I would rather recruit agents to sell life insurance like Bob and Eric used to do in the Midwest. Besides, I've used the value of my American Financial stock to borrow money and fund my divorce agreement with Mary. The kids have taken it pretty well—my visiting rights are very generous. It was expensive, but we ended up on good terms. I'll be spending more time with my son and the girls now than I could before the divorce. I want to stay right here in Northern California, sell life insurance and mutual funds, and make sure that my family grows together."

Fred smiled, sat back to listen, and tried to relax after Jim's speech. He lit another Marlboro. "I'm glad things are working well for you and your family, Jim. I hate to lose you at the national level, but I know you're comfortable working with Bob Green at American Pacific Life. I've been worried about you ever since you told me about the divorce. I know you're tired of the long-distance recruiting trips and want to get back to local recruiting, and that you want to develop new financial products for

Golden Gate Securities Company. You have to do what you think is best for you and your family. I would rather have you recruiting in California than losing you."

"Thanks, Fred. I knew I could count on you. I'll keep on recruiting locally, and I will support the vote for the joint venture." Fred had floated the idea of Real Estate Investment Trusts (REITs) with Bill Bretton when the two spent time together in New York. Both men thought United Express' Wall Street brokerage firm, Levy Loeb Rhodes, could feed Marty what he needed to move into the REIT arena. Fred knew that would be enough to hold Marty Cohen at American Financial.

Marty met with Fred in Fred's office, and admitted that he had been planning to accept the second bid if Midwest Financial went that far. "I wanted to take the cash and get my company back," he confessed. "But I like this new arrangement you've planned with United Express. It opens a whole new playing field for Cohen & Company. Through a joint venture, I can get into the REIT business faster. A REIT allows investors the chance to own shares in commercial real estate with access to dividend income and total returns. That would be more difficult on my own. I can see a whole new market if I worked with Levy Loeb Rhodes Brokerage Company through the joint venture."

Fred was determined. Since its introduction to the American Financial family, Cohen & Company had expanded at a rapid rate. The pieces had come together with a smoothness that impressed Fred. He was delighted that Marty would have no more thoughts of going back on his own. This would put American Financial in a strong position among conglomerates.

***

Bill Bretton flew in from New York with his financial team. They met with Fred, Bud Johnson, and Rick Taylor at Wood Island, and reviewed the proposed joint venture agreement in detail. It would be named American United Financial Partners, a California joint venture. Each party would contribute $100,000 as its initial capital. The joint venture was not a public company, and The Securities and Exchange Commission required no separate filing. David Walsh and Company reviewed the documents for American Financial.

Bud was concerned. He knew that the company was still short of long term capital—a problem since day one.

Back in New York, Howard Roberts was dealing with some issues of his own. He phoned Bill Bretton and told him that the board had become uncomfortable with the joint venture proposal. "They feel it promotes a new financial service that doesn't exist yet—financial planning for individuals in mid-America. Bill, I tried to convince the board this was not just a sojourn into the financial services industry—that it would be our step to broaden our commitment as America's national financial payments company. I had a call from John Barton, the same board member who had questioned it from the beginning. He called me after you left for San Francisco. I argued with him yesterday afternoon, to no avail. I'm afraid we've put Fred Maloney in a difficult position."

"It will be quite a shock, for sure, Howard. I know they need to stretch to come up with the

$100,000 for their share of the joint venture. They are still looking long-term financing, after the Equity Funding shock."

"I would not like to see Fred stumble from his financial planning goals. How much long-term capital do you think they are looking for, Bill?"

"From what I've seen of their financial statements, and listening to Fred's plans for introducing financial planning to his sales force, my guess would be something in the neighborhood of half a million. You know Fred won't sell the company, and it's too soon for another public stock offering. Charles De Long has just had the rug pulled out from under him on his plans for a second, ten percent proxy fight. American Financial doesn't have much in the way of collateral for a long-term bond. I'll look closer while I am here."

When Bill gave Fred the bad news, face to face, at Fred's office, Fred's face turned crimson. Fred's face flushed with anger. His right hand trembled, and his Cross pen fell to the floor. "What!" You've got to be kidding. Howard said he had an okay from his board." Fred reached for the nearest chair and slumped down into it, his legs spread apart.

"It was just as much of a surprise to Howard as it is to you, Fred."

Fred struggled back to his feet "That's for sure, Bill. But that's not what really hurts. We could have had a marriage made in heaven." Fred wondered how he would explain this to the others. "I guess Jim was right again, Bill. I should have checked all the facts before I reached a decision. We get to keep the Company, and we are free to run. But we don't have enough money to pursue two marketing plans."

"Howard feels bad, Fred, both as an American Financial shareholder and as a friend. He still thinks you are on the right track."

"Yeah—-on the right track with no train. I can't do this by myself."

Fred paused, picked up his Cross pen, lit a Marlboro, and responded. "Yes, we're still looking for some long-term financing to continue our expansion. But the Joint Venture that we came up with was the perfect vehicle for us to advance financial planning."

Fred called Rick with the bad news. Rick said he would be right over.

***

When Rick arrived and heard the full story from Fred and Bill Bretton, he agreed with the need for debt capital. "Even though this economy hasn't completed its recovery path yet, there is talk in Washington that the economy will turn around in the 1980s. American Financial needs capital to ride it through. Even though our stock is doing well, this is not a good time to be selling new shares of stock. The company had nothing but hopes for the future that could be pledged as collateral for a ten-year bond. Besides, interest rates were too high at this time."

Bill turned to Fred. "Would you be interested in a convertible debenture?"

Rick grasped for the opening. He pinched himself to make sure he was hearing what Bill was suggesting "That is something that would work well for us right now, Bill."

Fred asked "Why do you think so, Rick?"

"Fred, if we issued a convertible debenture now, we could shave a few basis points from the interest we would have to pay on a conventional bond. Convertible debentures do not normally require collateral for that bond, but a convertible debenture would have to provide for conversion of the debt into our common stock at maturity—-at a conversion price below the possibly higher current market value of our stock when the bond became due and payable."

Fred saw where Rick was headed. "You mean if we put the new capital from the bond to good use, and our stock appreciates by the time the bond is due to be repaid, the cash due on the bond at could then be repaid with our stock, instead of by using our cash?

"That's right, Fred" Rick assured him.

Following a long meeting between the three of them in Fred's office, Bill concluded "We are already a significant stockholder, Fred. We have an interest in buying a convertible venture from you. Let me talk to Howard about it."

The Company issued a $500,000 convertible debenture to United Express, interest payable quarterly at the prime rate. The conversion price was a five percent discount to the current market value of American Financial stock. It would be a ten-year bond, payable in cash or convertible to American Financial stock late in the 1980s. There would be no collateral required.

Fred was grateful to Providence. The Company reached out to middle-America; *"We lost Marco, but Susan, and Marco's family, will prosper. Mark Twain had it right. "We will not have to lament the things that we did not try"*

CHAPTER TWELVE
The Vision

The race had been a long one, but the wind was astern now. Smooth sailing lay ahead. The ripples on the water gave way to stronger winds, as Fred took on the titans of the financial industry— fiduciary duty was his first mate. The tepid economic atmosphere came back to life in the twenty-first century.

Fred Maloney took his conglomerate into the mainstream. American Financial took the lead as it introduced financial planning to the country. It became the lynchpin for financial services; its common stock achieved listing on the American Stock Exchange.

Jim and Mary Barns were remarried, and they welcomed another baby. Jim settled down and decided to focus on recruiting for American Pacific

Life in California. He remained on the board of directors of American Financial as its board was enlarged to include Keith Raab and Frank Gavin.

Rick Taylor became a successful trial lawyer with Woodford and Hoskins. He then opened his own law office at Wood Island in Greenbrae. He focused on retirement and estate planning for clients throughout Northern California.

Marty Cohen kept his primary office in Long Beach as he moved into the REIT arena with new products. He had established a rapport with Levy Loeb Rhodes at the United Express Company.

Susan Flynn grew closer to her father. As her children moved toward maturity, she was able to provide sufficient financial resources for their education. She often reminded them of the acumen their father provided in the creation of American Financial.

Epilogue

It would be two decades before financial advisers consistently met the standard of putting the best interests of their clients above their own when managing client finances. Today, Registered Financial Advisors and Certified Financial Planners do much more than just giving investment advice.

A national association of financial planners, with its standards for licensing and ethics, came into being. Bringing all the pieces of one's economic life together is a challenging task. From budgeting to planning for retirement, saving for education, managing taxes, and providing life insurance coverage, the word "finances" no longer has a single definition.

Certified Financial Planners™ (CFP) is an essential resource for customers. CFPs must complete extensive training and meet experience requirements to achieve the designation of CFP. They are held to rigorous ethical standards.

President Barack Obama said, "It's a straightforward principle: You want to give financial advice, you've got to put your clients' interests first."

It would be forty years before major brokerages and investment advisers in the United States changed their advertising to emphasize fees for financial planning advice rather than just relying on commissions for securities transactions.

In the first decade of the twenty-first century, discount broker Charles Schwab cut fees and commissions across the board, targeting middle-class customers for commission-free exchange-traded funds—mutual funds that trade like stocks (ETFs). Wall Street brokerages started offering services at rock-bottom prices. In 2019, Schwab's client assets dwarfed those at Bank of America. Merrill Lynch, Morgan Stanley's brokerage arm, and the UBS Group AG's Americas unit combined. Fidelity and Vanguard offered commission-free ETFs.

In 2015, a *Wall Street Journal* editorial advocated that registered investment advisers act in their clients' best interests.

A June 6, 2019 report in the *Business and Finance* section of the Wall Street Journal states that "Stock brokers will have more responsibility to act in the best interest or investors and tell them about conflicts of interest that can skew advice under a regulation approved Wednesday."

Note: A story of the Equity Funding Corporation of America financial fraud, *Billion Dollar Bubble,* was made into a television movie in 1978. This author has not seen that movie.

Postscript

The following was taken from the archives of *The New York Times.*

"Insurance Fraud Charged by S.E.C. to Equity Funding"

By Robert J. Cole

April 4, 1973

The Equity Funding Corporation of America, once the darling of institutional investors, signed a consent decree with the Federal Government yesterday in the wake of a widening scandal that may involve the sale of millions of dollars of fraudulent insurance policies.

Meanwhile, a consortium of leading New York and West Coast banks led by the First National City Bank of New York, which had lent the company more than $50 million, served notice last night that it was demanding "accelerated payment" of the debt, according to a company spokesman.

Earlier yesterday, the New York Stock Exchange began an intensive investigation of trading in Equity Funding stock in the last few weeks to determine whether insiders had engaged in illegal trading before reports of widespread financial irregularities became public knowledge.

Difficulties Were Reported

The Big Board, halted trading in Equity Funding stock last Tuesday after rumors spread of significant financial difficulties and institutional holders of the stock dumped huge blocks.

The Fraud charges, which may lead to substantial losses by brokerage firms, banks, and other institutions not yet identified, prompted Equity Funding to settle yesterday with the Securities and Exchange Commission. The surprise consent decree was obtained on the same day that the S.E.C. had filed its charges in United States District Court in Los Angeles.

The Government agency, according to an Equity Funding press release, had charged the company—a financial services complex with interests in insurance, mutual funds and tax shelters—with major violations of Federal securities laws and a "scheme" to inflate the company's financial statements through the creation of nonexistent insurance business and bogus assets.

Sources close to the Government said the Commission "did not get everything it asked in to reach settlement yesterday with the Securities and Exchange Commission.

The surprise consent decrees were obtained on the same day that the S.E.C. had filed its charges in United States District Court in Los Angeles.

Moving to protect company stockholders and policyholders of a subsidiary, the Equity Funding Insurance Company, now under scrutiny by several state and federal agencies, the S.E.C. also obtained a permanent injunction to prevent further violations.

Note: April 4, 1973, *New York Times* article continued from the above duplication.

Glossary

Bear Market is a stock market where prices for securities are falling or are expected to fall. It is the opposite of a Bull Market.

Conglomerate is a large corporation run as a single business, but made up of several firms or corporations suppling diverse goods and/or services.

Convertible debenture is a type of long-term debt issued by a company that can be converted into stock after a specified period. Convertible debentures are usually unsecured bonds or loans, which means there is no underlying collateral connected to the debt. These long-term debt securities pay interest returns to the bondholder, who is the lender. The unique feature of convertible debentures is that they are convertible into stock at specified times. This feature gives the bondholder security that may offset the risk involved with investing in unsecured debt.

Financial planning means to do more than simply advising on available investments. Whether providing help on budgeting, retirement planning, education savings, insurance coverage, or even tax-optimization strategy, financial planning means much more than just investing.

Funding is the lending of funds to a person to cover the cost of his life insurance premiums. Premium finance loans can be provided or guaranteed by a third party. Insurance companies occasionally provide premium financing services through their premium finance platforms. Premium financing is mainly devoted to financing life insurance, which differs from property and casualty insurance.

Initial Public Offering (IPO) is the process of offering shares of a private corporation to the public for the first time. Growing companies that need capital will frequently use IPOs to raise money.

Fixed exchange rate is a type of exchange regime in which a currency's value is fixed against either the value of another single currency, a basket of other currencies, or another measure of value, such as gold.

Mutual Fund is an investment program funded by shareholders that trades in diversified holdings and is professionally managed. A **No Load Mutual Fund** is a mutual fund in which shares are sold without a commission or sales charge. This absence of fees occurs because the shares are distributed directly by the investment company, instead of going through a secondary party.

Overwrite income is a commission paid to an agent or broker on business sold by subagents in his or her territory.

Public offering is the offering of securities of a company to the public. Generally, the securities are to be listed on a stock exchange. A public offering requires the issuing company to publish a prospectus detailing the terms and rights attached to the offered security, as well as information on the company itself and its finances.

Real Estate Investment Trust (REIT) is a company that owns, operates or finances income-producing real estate. Modeled after mutual funds, REITs provide all investors the chance to own valuable real estate, present the opportunity to access dividend-based income and total returns, and help communities grow, thrive and revitalize.

Reinsurance is insurance that is purchased by an insurance company, in which some part of its own insurance liabilities is passed on ("ceded") to another insurance company

67763441R00205

Made in the USA
Columbia, SC
01 August 2019